Though born in Ohio, Miss Darcy is very much at home in her special world, Regency England. So much so that readers of her novels find it hard not to believe that she was born and reared in the best Society of that day. Romantic, gay, intriguing, her books are enchanting delights.

Other books by Clare Darcy:

CRESSIDA
EUGENIA
REGINA
ELYZA

Clare Darcy

Rolande

A Troubadour Spectacular

Futura Publications Limited

A Troubadour Book

First published in Great Britain by
Futura Publications Limited 1980

ISBN : 0 7088 1897 8

Printed in Great Britain by
Hunt Barnard Printing Ltd., Aylesbury, Bucks.

Futura Publications Limited,
110 Warner Road,
Camberwell, London SE5

ONE

Mr. Jasper Carrington, arriving on a June evening at his aunt's slim house in Half Moon Street at an hour at which many of the guests who had been invited to her musical soirée had already begun to leave, found himself accosted at the head of the staircase by his cousin, the Baroness Lebanoff, and dragged off by her with a cry of surprise and delight into a small saloon which had served as the refreshment room, but was now inhabited only by a pair of gorgeous but dispirited footmen, presiding over a much depleted table.

"Go away, go away — do!" the Baroness addressed them, waving an imperious hand, clad in an expensive blossom-pink glove of French kid, and flinging her taffeta cloak down upon the nearest convenient chair.

Most people did as they were told when the Baroness addressed them in that autocratic tone and fixed them with the unwinking stare of her bright dark eyes, which were as unconcerned with any objections

1

that might conceivably be raised as if they had been set in the head of one of the brilliant tropical birds of the parrot family to which she bore a strong resemblance.

The footmen were no exception to this rule. They regarded each other, came to a mutual agreement, and silently deserted their posts.

"Good!" said the Baroness, seating herself upon the chair next the one on which she had flung her cloak. "Now we can have a really *comfortable* cose. Dearest Jasper, have you just arrived in town? I heard you were in Vienna and I wrote you *several* letters, which I am *quite* sure you will tell me you did not receive. If you do, I shall scream, because it is all very complicated and I cannot bear to tell the same story twice. It seems so dreadfully uninventive!"

The Baroness was of Mr. Carrington's mother's generation, not his own, being over fifty, while Mr. Carrington himself had yet to attain his thirtieth year. Mr. Carrington was such a handsome, self-possessed, easy gentleman, with his tall figure showing to such excellent advantage in a coat of Bath superfine that was undoubtedly one of Weston's masterpieces, his snowy cravat tied with such devilish skill, and his smile mirrored with such lazily amused charm in his cool grey eyes, that even had he told the Baroness he had not received a single one of her letters she would no doubt have contrived to refrain from screaming. Women in general found Mr. Carrington irresistible, the combination of a ruthlessly — not to say at times rudely — autocratic nature and a generally good-humoured manner was not at all what they were accustomed to.

However, he said nothing of the sort to the

Baroness about not having received her letters but instead sat down beside her and asked why she thought he had come back to England when the Season was all but over and it would be several months before the hunting began.

'"Because you *have* received my letters, and so you know about the Imposter,"' the Baroness said, looking immensely gratified. "I *know* it is a very dull time of year, dearest Jasper, but — eight million pounds! One would really do anything for *that*!"

"Even murder?" enquired Jasper. "I have been considering that."

"Oh, quite definitely murder!" The Baroness tapped his arm briskly with her fan, a pretty piece of hand-painted parchment and Arles lace on ivory sticks, with a classical subject. "Only it is really your aunt Honoria who should be your victim, not this vapid boy she has picked up to pass off as Giles Arcourt — though *he* is most certainly murderable, too, if that is a proper word. All pink cheeks and fair hair and sly angel's eyes, with one of those *gluey* voices Austrians so often have."

"*Is* he an imposter?" Jasper asked.

"My dear, but of course! I never had a great deal of use for John Arcourt, but neither he nor that French woman he married could possibly have spawned such a sugar-candy object as this! *She* was far too tall, and not precisely plain, you know, but certainly not beautiful — but she had an elegance, an unmistakable air of *ton* — "

"In other words," Jasper helped her out, "you think my dear aunt Honoria, while perhaps not quite

3

prepared to commit murder to obtain eight million pounds, is perfectly willing to commit any crime short of it in order to attain her diabolical ends?''

''Well, they *are* diabolical, dear boy,'' said the Baroness, ''as you yourself must be the first to admit, no matter how *nonchalamment* you choose to take it. Here we have all been thinking for ages that you would be as rich as Croesus as soon as that absurd Will was finally wound up, for heaven knows, no-one could ever have imagined finding a small child after it had been lost for fourteen years. God knows how much you have borrowed on the head of it — enough to ruin every moneylender in London, I daresay! And now, just when a judgement is expected at last — or at least it is expected, I understand, as soon as the Court begins sitting next term — here comes Honoria, or, rather, that odious man of business of hers, Croil, claiming to have discovered, after all this time, people of the name of Schmidt to whom the child was entrusted by the Dubruls before they died. *And* they have produced all sorts of documents to bolster their claim — the Court of Chancery is mad about documents, you know! — to say nothing of an opal ring that Honoria swears she gave John Arcourt before he went to France. Haven't I always said that opals are unlucky?''

The will to which the Baroness referred was the famous Arcourt Will, which had been a *cause célèbre* in England since the seventeenth century, when John Arcourt, Gent., of Arcourt's Hall, Bucks., being on very bad terms with his son and heir, and having an even poorer opinion of his grandson, had conceived the brilliant idea of making a will in which he had stipulated that the entire fortune that had come to him through his second wife, a considerable heiress, was to be put in trust at interest for a hundred and fifty years, at the end of which time the accumulated sum would go to the Arcourt heir of that day.

Of course the whole matter had ended in the Court of Chancery, with each succeeding Arcourt heir over the generations attempting to break the Will, but without the least success. As a result of those perennially raised and disappointed expectations, Arcourt's Hall had been alternately expensively refurbished and allowed to fall to rack, so that it was, at present, in one of its periods of decline and almost uninhabitable. Jasper Carrington, to whom, as it was outside the scope of the Arcourt Will, ownership of the house had descended without legal difficulties, had never been able to afford to live there; and it was now almost shut up under the care of an elderly couple, its beautiful Restoration rooms breathing dust and mould and dim, enchanting memories of the past.

This state of affairs had never weighed very heavily upon Jasper, however, as he much preferred spending that portion of the year when he was not in London, or visiting friends in the Shires during the hunting season, in travels to such exotic quarters of the globe as Egypt, Syria, Turkey, and Greece, where he always succeeded in amusing himself very well, although not infrequently to the accompaniment of a certain degree of notoriety.

Moreover, as the direct heir in the male line to the Arcourt millions (John Arcourt's son Giles had vanished without a trace as a small child, after having been smuggled out of France into Austria during the period of turmoil when the French Wars had been resumed after the brief Peace of Amiens), Jasper had, for a good many years, been expecting that all his financial difficulties would be happily resolved when the Will was at last wound up and under its terms he, as the son of John Arcourt's elder sister, Isabella, would inherit a fortune which now amounted to eight million pounds. It was therefore no good denying, in spite of his well-deserved reputation for an unshakable urbanity, that the news contained in the Baroness's letters that his aunt Honoria had finally run the missing Giles Arcourt to earth, had come as a very nasty shock. Jasper, who was then in Vienna, had forthwith come on to London, not without some ideas of his own, he now confided to the Baroness, as to how to cope with the situation.

"You see, I have had the most extraordinary piece of luck," he told her. "There is a girl —"

The Baroness tapped his arm reprovingly with her fan.

"Dearest Jasper, with eight million pounds at stake, I *do* think you might forget your petticoat-affairs for just a *short* time," she said to him.

"But it's nothing of the sort," protested Jasper. "In point of fact, she's not in my style in the least. Tall girl, figure like a boy's — and *that's* just the point — and she even has that dark-coppery hair —"

"*What* dark-coppery hair?"

"I beg your pardon. I'm being carried away. But before I enter upon tedious explanations — are you *quite* sure that this lad Aunt Honoria has produced really *is* an imposter? There is not the slightest particle of use in my even beginning upon all this, you know, if it is going to turn out that he is the *bona fide* Giles, miraculously restored after all these years to the bosom of his family."

"Of course I am sure," said the Baroness, whose ·code it was never to entertain doubts. "You know as well as I do that Honoria has been casting about for years for some way to cut you out of the inheritance and get it all for herself instead — or, rather, for her dear boy Geraint, which comes to the same thing in the end. Go away!" she broke off to call imperiously to a solitary, bemused-looking guest who, apparently unable to endure any longer the piercing soprano voice that was still to be heard warbling away with fiendish persistence in another room, came wandering in at the door with a glazed eye fixed upon the deserted refreshment table. "Go away! It's all gone!"

She waved her fan at him as Jasper had seen farmwives shooing hens, and he vanished, disappointed.

"That is old General Pusey," she remarked. "He was attached to the Embassy in Petersburg while my poor Lebanoff was still alive, and tried repeatedly to seduce me. Now where was I? Oh yes — Honoria. I have known that look of hers ever since I was four years old and she and your mama came to visit me in the nursery. She *always* knew what she wanted, and never failed to get it, looking all the while as prim and proper as a pattern-card of virtue. I daresay it is because she is so small that she is never suspected of anything, but I could tell you tales about her that would make your blood run cold. Did you know, for instance, that poor Lord Prest was madly in love with a girl named Radnor and had every intention of offering for her until

Honoria stepped into the picture and blackened her character to such an extent that he ended by offering for Honoria instead?"

"No, I didn't" said Jasper. "He left her quite well to pass, too, didn't he? Why is she so set on having my eight million pounds?"

"She loathes you, of course. You are everything poor Geraint isn't — charming, intelligent, a nonpareil in every sport, an arbiter of fashion, to name but a few of your many accomplishments — and she is determined he shall outshine you in one point, at least. Besides, she is greedy."

Jasper remarked that that was all very well, but that Lady Prest must be very sure she could lay her hands on the dibs after she had managed to persuade the Court to turn them over to the bogus Giles Arcourt, or she would never have gone to so much trouble.

"Well, of course she is sure," said the Baroness. "She can always threaten to expose him as an imposter, you know, if he does not do exactly as she tells him. That is why I am so positive that he *is* an imposter. Otherwise, there would be no point in her doing all this."

"On the other hand," Jasper remarked, "Birdwhistell says the Court may very well be inclined to the point of view that the boy *is* the genuine article, no matter how skeptical he is himself about the boy's having any Arcourt blood in him and over the validity of his claim."

"Oh, you've seen Birdwhistell, have you? Dear boy, he says that because he is a solicitor, and solicitors are quite as mad over documents as Courts are; they

8

simply cannot help themselves. What they don't know is Honoria. She is well enough off to bribe half a dozen Viennese families named Schmidt to sign affidavits swearing they were the couple to whom those unfortunate Dubruls gave the child, and I make no doubt that is exactly what she has done."

"Well, two can play at that game," said Jasper thoughtfully. "And what is more, if I can make sure of all you say, they probably will. That is where this extraordinary girl enters the picture. She is an actress, you see —"

"Yes, I know all about your actresses, dearest Jasper," said the Baroness with an air of resignation. "I am *not* interested in them at present."

"You'd be interested in this one if you could see her," Jasper said. "She looks enough like that portrait in the Ivory Saloon at Arcourt's Hall of John Arcourt's French bride — coppery hair and all — to be her sister. Also, when wearing breeches, her son, if you are following me. I've already told you she has a figure like a boy's, and she does breeches parts *à merveille*. Most important of all, she is obviously quite out of her element in the third-rate travelling company in Calais that rejoices in her services at present, and I imagine would be amenable to a lucrative offer of honest work of almost any sort."

The Baroness, for once fairly startled into silence, stared at him.

"You *don't* mean — ?" she said, after a moment.

"Yes, I do," said Jasper. "No one, seeing her dressed for the part, would guess she was not a youth of seventeen. Actually, I should put her age at nearer

9

twenty; she does what she is doing far too well for seventeen. Her name, by the way, is Miss Henry — half English, I should imagine, and speaks German, as I was able to discover by discreet enquiry (I have never met her socially, you understand), with an Austrian accent. What, dearest Louisa, do you think Croil and all those learned gentlemen of the Court of Chancery will say if I suddenly turn up with my own Giles Arcourt, resembling his much-lamented mama so very strikingly that he will make *their* candidate look nohow?''

"Dearest Jasper," breathed the Baroness, recovering herself and beaming with admiration, "you wouldn't dare!"

"Wouldn't I?" retorted Jasper, and at that moment his aunt, Lady Prest, followed by her son Geraint, her widowed niece, Mrs. Falkirk, and a very young, fair man with delicately moulded features but a rather lumpish manner, walked into the room.

"General Pusey told me I should find you here," said Lady Prest, at once approaching Jasper and holding out both hands to him with a gracious smile that gave no hint that her feelings towards him were as the Baroness had described them. "How very naughty of you, Jasper dear, to come back to London and not let me know! We all thought you were on your way to Buda!"

Honoria, the Dowager Lady Prest, was a very small woman, but she carried herself so regally erect that, as her cousin the Baroness had once remarked of her, she always gave one the impression that she expected one to rise and curtsey when she came into the room. She had once been a Beauty and still had the air of careless command that most Beauties relinquish in petulance and chagrin at about the age of forty.

The fact that she had managed to retain it when she was well past fifty was perhaps owing to her being an absolute ruler in her own family circle. Her orphaned niece Peggy had, when a beautiful, meltingly fair girl of eighteen, married at her behest a middle-aged gentleman who had had the advantage of inheriting shortly before that time one of the largest fortunes in Lancashire. He had subsequently managed, by heroic effort, to dissipate almost all of it before dying some ten years after the marriage date, and Peggy Falkirk was now an impecunious widow existing upon her aunt's charity and obliged to hear every day how it was her own weak-mindedness and nothing else that had allowed the late Mr. Falkirk to pursue an untrammelled way to financial disaster.

As for Geraint, Lady Prest's son, who had only recently attained his majority, he had been at once so cosseted and so confined by his imperious and adoring mama that he was generally considered an intolerable milksop, in spite of his undoubted good looks and considerable natural abilities. He was a dark, handsome young man with a self-effacing manner and very little to say for himself, and he had always hopelessly envied and admired his cousin Jasper.

Lady Prest, having managed to convict Jasper of rag-manners because he had come uninvited to her soirée and had allowed himself to be drawn off by the Baroness instead of seeking his hostess out at once, now followed up her advantage by introducing him to his "cousin," .the presumed Giles Arcourt — "who has

11

been restored to us," she went on, with entire aplomb, "by an amazing Act of Providence. I daresay dear Louisa has told you all about it?"

Jasper, who was scrutinising the lumpish youth with a lazily detached air, said, as he shook hands with him, that the Baroness had perhaps not expressed it in quite those terms. Upon this, the youth, speaking with a pronounced Austrian accent and evidently terrified of Jasper's quite civil but candidly observant gaze, glanced at Lady Prest and then said in obvious alarm that he was very happy to make the gentleman's acquaintance.

"You must call him Jasper, Giles dear," said Lady Prest sweetly. "He is your cousin, and I am sure is prepared to be very fond of you as soon as he has got over his first natural chagrin at learning that he is not to inherit the Arcourt fortune."

"Chagrin," said Jasper, who had now completed his survey of the Arcourt pretender, "is scarcely the *mot juste*, I believe, dear Aunt. I should say, rather, incredulity — or at least, suspended belief. I hear you have collected a very impressive set of documents in support of this young man's case. I suggest that you allow Birdwhistell to examine them, and I may then come to some definite conclusion as to whether to welcome him into the family."

He turned to Peggy Falkirk, who was a great friend of his and, indeed, had been hopelessly in love with him for years, along with a number of other ladies, none of whom had ever succeeded in rousing the slightest wish in his heart (if he had one, which they considered debatable) to abandon his bachelor estate. But Lady Prest, who, like Royalty, never considered a conversation at an end until she had ended it herself, interrupted him at once and said she hoped he did not intend to be disagreeable.

"I am never disagreeable," said Jasper, which was a highly inaccurate statement, for he was disagreeable whenever he felt like it, but almost always without malice, so that he rarely offended. "But I have a very cautious nature, ma'am. And when there is a matter of eight million pounds involved, I am sorry to say that my cautious nature quite gets the better of me. Peggy," he went on, returning to Mrs. Falkirk, "your eyes have become, if possible, even larger and bluer than they were the last time I saw you."

Mrs. Falkirk, who, though nine-and-twenty, could still blush, did so charmingly, but, with a nervous glance at her aunt, said she was past the age for compliments.

"Well, so am not I," said the Baroness frankly, "which is why I am off for Paris next week. Will you come with me, Peggy dear? I can promise you baskets of compliments, all of them more graceful than any you will ever have from Jasper. He is far too lazy to spend sufficient time thinking them up to do them properly."

Peggy said, with still more marked symptoms of nervousness, that she was afraid her aunt could not spare her just then, and Lady Prest, who appeared to feel that they had got off the subject, asked Jasper in a tone of disapproval whether he intended to remain in London for the present.

"Oh, I rather think not," said Jasper, with his customary vagueness over his future movements, which had frequently caused his friends and relations to write

2

to him in Leicestershire when he was actually on his way to Cairo. "There are a few things I shall have to see to — in various places, I think."

Lady Prest, who had expected him to be more difficult about the sudden appearance upon the scene of "Giles Arcourt," felt that there was something sinister in his restraint and gave him a cold, penetrating look, wondering what he was up to.

As for the Baroness, who knew very well what he was up to, she decided instantly that she would even postpone her visit to Paris, if necessary, in order to be the first to make the acquaintance of the mysterious Miss Henry, who she did not doubt would be brought into the picture by Jasper as soon as he was, so to speak, able to lay his hands upon her.

TWO

As a result of this decision, the Baroness found hereself seated, on a rainy evening some ten days later, in a private parlour of the Ship Inn in Dover, inspecting, along with Jasper, the young woman who had just arrived by the packet from Calais and announced herself as Miss Rolande Henry.

The first thing that occurred to her as she sat looking at Miss Henry's tall, slender, and undeniably graceful figure, clad in a rather damp duffle cloak and a deplorable hat, was that Jasper had been quite correct when he had stated that she was not the type of girl he admired. Jasper, when he found time to tear his attention away from horses, sporting events, and the latest fashion in cravats, admired meltingly blue-eyed blondes of a classical turn of countenance, like Peggy Falkirk, and all the High Flyers he had ever been known to have had in keeping had rigidly conformed to these specifications.

Miss Henry, on the contrary, possessed a mass of

thick, dark-coppery curls, the piquant features of what the French denominate a *jolie laide*, and a pair of blue eyes which were full of a blazing sincerity and had undoubtedly never melted in their owner's life.

On the other hand, the Baroness decided, she definitely did resemble the portrait of the late Mrs. John Arcourt in the Ivory Saloon at Arcourt's Hall. The resemblance became particularly striking when Miss Henry's eyes fell upon Jasper and her features assumed the expression of somewhat wary hauteur which the artist (it was Reynolds, but unfortunately not one of his better efforts) had immortalised upon Mrs. Arcourt's face.

"Oh!" said Miss Henry as she took in Jasper's elegant figure, quizzically surveying glance, and obvious air of man-about-townishness. "I thought you would be a — an older gentleman." Her eyes then fell upon the Baroness, unmistakably the lady of fashion from the top of her modishly coiffed head to her bronze kid half-boots. "And who is this?" she demanded.

"My cousin, the Baroness Lebanoff," said Jasper, noting with approval that Miss Henry spoke English without an accent, only the excellence of her diction suggesting that it was not her mother tongue. Jasper himself spoke several languages, but rarely used them except when absolutely necessary, having a rooted dislike to exerting anything but the minimum effort in dealing with life. "She has kindly consented to be present at this interview," he said. "I thought it might make matters more comfortable for you. Won't you sit down, Miss Henry?"

Miss Henry sat down. She was — very surprisingly,

the Baroness considered — obviously a lady, though she had none of the airs and graces of one, and, indeed, seemed determined not to do or say anything that might cause it to appear that she considered herself in any way above the position for which she was being interviewed. That that position was one in a theatrical company was soon made embarrassingly clear, and the Baroness, who had been wondering by what means Jasper had induced her to drop everything and come pelting over to England, gazed at him indignantly. She felt herself drawn at once to Miss Henry, who appeared to have a character quite as strong and forthright as her own, and she determined on the spot to do everything in her power to see to it that Jasper's habit of striding heedlessly through life straight towards his current goal, scattering people like bric-à-brac, did not cause her any undue inconvenience.

It was, of course, necessary to explain to Miss Henry at once the rather peculiar reason for which she had been summoned to England. But Jasper, displaying what the Baroness considered was, for him, unusual tact, ascertained first that Miss Henry had not dined and, summoning a waiter, ordered the most appealing meal that could be provided on short notice, which turned out to be a dish of mutton steaks and cucumber.

When this had been brought, together with a basket of damson tartlets, and Miss Henry had divested herself of her wet cloak and unmodish hat to the decided improvement of her appearance, Jasper abandoned the laborious conversation of commonplaces with which he had been attempting to convince her that he was an entirely trustworthy, not to say perfectly ordinary, sort of fellow and the Baroness a lady of the highest rank and reputation instead of the proprietress of a fashionable bagnio, which Miss Henry apparently suspected her of being, and began in a roundabout way to enquire into her history and antecedents. Obviously it would not do, he had told the Baroness as they had been travelling down to Dover together, to attempt to employ the girl if she was going to turn out to have a mother who followed her about like a dragon, which he had had a vague feeling, from the two evenings he had spent watching Miss Henry perform in a very unattractive theatre in Calais while waiting for the weather to clear sufficiently for the Channel packet to leave, might be the case.

But it now appeared that there was no mother in the picture. Miss Henry, who had a very good appetite and evidently found mutton steaks to her liking, was sufficiently mollified by them to answer a few enquiries about herself, stating briefly that she was an orphan, English on her father's side and French on her mother's, that she had been born in France but had spent her youth in extensive travel all over Europe. This had come about because her father, a former officer in the Dragoon Guards (here Jasper's brows went up skeptically), had supported his family either by selling his sword to a foreign prince or by making use of his considerable equestrian skill to engage in exhibitions of a theatrical nature, such as she understood were to be viewed in England at Astley's Amphitheatre.

Pressed for further details, however, she baulked, and, looking up at Jasper in the act of attacking one of the damson tartlets, said to him severely, "I think it would be a great deal better, Mr. Carrington, if you told me now exactly *where* your theatrical company is at present, and *what* parts you would like me to play."

"Well, it's not a theatrical company, you see," Jasper admitted, rapidly but quite without embarrassment. "You see, I rather thought it might put you off if I wrote you it was actually something rather different that I had in mind."

Miss Henry laid down her knife and fork.

"I thought as much," she said, with a good deal of emphasis and ineffable scorn in her voice. She got up. "In fact," she went on, crossing the room quickly to retrieve her hat and cloak, "I was sure of it as soon as I set eyes on you, Mr. Carrington. *You* a theatrical manager!" She crammed the deplorable hat down on her coppery curls with a fine disregard for effect and faced Jasper bitterly. "I will have you know, sir," she said, "that I am *not* that kind of young woman. And as for you, madam," she went on, rounding suddenly upon the Baroness, "all I can say is that if you really are a baroness, you might find better use for your time than spending it luring honest young women into the traps this — this *viper* has laid for them!"

The Baroness was so fascinated by this sudden attack that for the moment she could find nothing to say or do, but Jasper, moving with what was for him unusual celerity, immediately rose and placed himself between Miss Henry and the door.

"If you will attend to me for one moment — " he began; but Miss Henry, regarding him in a very unfriendly manner, at once informed him that if he did not move aside at once and let her pass she would cry out for help.

"*Most* unwise, my dear," said the Baroness, who had by now recovered her usual poise and came philanthropically to Jasper's assistance. "If you refuse to stay and listen to him you will be throwing away a really splendid opportunity to earn an honest ten thousand pounds — I believe that *was* the sum you mentioned, dearest Jasper? — as well as to help poor Mr. Carrington not to be swindled out of eight million pounds that rightfully belongs to him. You see, all he *really* wishes you to do is to pretend to be his cousin for a while, Giles Arcourt, who is a boy, of course, but I understand you are perfectly splendid in breeches parts, and then your resemblance to Giles's mama is quite extraordinarily striking —"

Not unnaturally, Miss Henry appeared to be somewhat bewildered by this speech, but it had at least the effect of causing her to assume a less threatening attitude towards Jasper. He at once took advantage of this to offer her another damson tartlet.

"Do be reasonable, Miss Henry," he said persuasively — and there were young women all over Europe and several other continents who could attest to the fact that when Jasper Carrington wished to be persuasive he could be very persuasive indeed. "After all, you have come all this way, and the least you can do is listen to me before you go back to that revolting company I found you in — *if* you still want to go then, which I very much doubt. I assure you, the whole thing is perfectly respectable —"

Miss Henry said darkly that she saw nothing respectable about bringing people into strange countries under false pretences, but consented to sit down again and eat damson tartlets while attending as Jasper explained the intricacies of the Arcourt Will and his plan for thwarting Lady Prest's scheme to obtain his eight million pounds for her protégé. She listened closely, although in no way slighting the damson tartlets, and when he had finished said at once, decidedly, "I think that is the silliest plan I have ever heard of. No one in his right mind would believe I was a boy."

"Of course they would," said Jasper, stung by this cavalier criticism out of his intention to be civil and agreeable. "I'd have believed it myself when I saw you playing at Calais, if you hadn't been set down as *Mademoiselle Henry* in the playbill. You had none of the mannerisms of a female while you were acting the part —"

And not many now, he would have continued if tact had not restrained him; for in point of fact Miss Henry moved and spoke with a boyish freedom that made it appear improbable that she had ever been confined in anything like the narrow circle of conventional behaviour that was considered proper for an English young lady.

Miss Henry, however, continued to look unconvinced, and said they would no doubt all be taken up by the Authorities if they were to try to carry out so harebrained a scheme. She had heard, she said, that the Authorities were very severe in England.

"Nonsense!" said Jasper. "There isn't the least danger of that. If anyone begins to suspect you, you

21

merely become Miss Henry again and Giles Arcourt vanishes without a trace. I shan't want you to *remain* Giles Arcourt, at any rate, any longer than will be necessary to cast suspicion on my aunt's candidate and cause those bumbleheaded idiots in the Court of Chancery to take a closer look at his credentials. Once he has been exposed as an imposter, you will disappear, leaving me to admit with great regret that I, too, have been imposed upon by a bogus claimant — after which I shall legitimately inherit my eight million pounds and we shall all, except Aunt Honoria, of course, be as merry as grigs."

Miss Henry still looked unconvinced, but Jasper and the Baroness could see that she was wavering. After all, they both thought a trifle smugly, ten thousand pounds was ten thousand pounds.

But in thinking this, they were obviously misjudging her, for, having finished the last of the damson tartlets, she uttered an abrupt enquiry as to what guarantee they could give her that Jasper really would become the victim of a monstrous miscarriage of justice if she did not agrree to help him, thus proving that her mind had been running in an entirely different direction.

Jasper and the Baroness looked at each other.

"I could say I'd take you to see my solicitor, I expect," Jasper confessed after a moment, "only the thing is, he rather seems to be of the opinion that my aunt's candidate may possibly be the genuine article."

"*That* is because he is a fool," said the Baroness firmly. "All solicitors are. It comes from the necessity of being logical all day long. Life, you see, my child," she went on, turning to Miss Henry, "is not logical. Far from it. The most incredible things frequently turn out to be perfectly true, as in the case we now have under consideration. Unlikely as it seems, my cousin Honoria has embarked upon a scheme which no lady of breeding or conscience should associate herself with, and the consequence — if you do not step in to save him — will be that poor Mr. Carrington will be defrauded of all his substance and end his days as a pauper."

Jasper, who was beginning to rebel at figuring as "poor Mr. Carrington," protested that it was perhaps not quite so bad as that.

"Don't quibble," said the Baroness majestically. "Miss Henry has quite enough to assimilate as it is, without our going into unimportant details. None of the Carringtons has ever been provident, and it is not to be expected that you would be the first. On the other hand, I know of no one in the family who could put eight million pounds to better use. You have excellent taste and a generous nature, which is more than can be said of either Honoria or Geraint."

Miss Henry, who appeared to be still considering Jasper's reply to her question without paying a great deal of heed to the Baroness's intromission, said unexpectedly at this point that she was more inclined than not to believe that he really was the victim of injustice, because he had admitted that his solicitor considered that the Giles Arcourt his aunt had produced might possibly be the real one.

"People who are hardened deceivers," she said

with a slightly disillusioned air, "never admit to anything that does not further their deception. I have recently discovered that."

The Baroness and Jasper, both fascinated by this information, simultaneously enquired how.

"It was several months ago, just after *Maman* died," said Miss Henry, who appeared to be unbending slightly under the influence of the mutton steaks, the damson tartlets, a good fire in a cosy room on a wet evening, and her companions' obvious attention. "*Maman*, you see, was an actress, but she never wished me to follow in her footsteps, which was why I was sent to a *pensionnat* in Switzerland when I was fourteen, so that I could learn all the accomplishments proper to a lady and make a suitable marriage. Personally, I found it very uninteresting there, and in spite of my having all the accomplishments when I left, and Papa's being the son of baronet, no one wished to marry me — or at least no one whom *Maman* considered suitable in the least — "

She was interrupted at this point by the Baroness and Jasper, who repeated simultaneously, like a Greek chorus, "The son of a baronet?" The Baroness went on, as a solo, "But of course! The Northumberland Henrys! All quite mad, and there *was* a son, years ago, who left the army and married a French actress. Your papa, my dear?"

Miss Henry nodded.

"They are, I believe, all dead now," continued the Baroness, "or at least I haven't heard of them for years. There was used to be an elderly spinster who came to town every year for the Season in the most amazing costumes and kept a monkey, but she was drowned in a bathing-machine at Brighton. I believe the title went to a very distant cousin last year when Sir Peregrine, who must have been at least ninety, died."

Miss Henry nodded once more. "My grandpapa," she said gloomily. 'He and Papa didn't get on."

"And your papa is dead now as well?"

"Oh, yes. Since three years," said Miss Henry; who, in spite of her excellent English, was occasionally betrayed into a continentalism. "After that, *Maman* said it would be best perhaps if we went to England and had a small conversation with Sir Peregrine, but he was not encouraging when she wrote to him — in fact, he did not reply at all — so we did not go."

The Baroness and Jasper uttered sympathetic murmurs.

"But that was not what I began to tell you," said Miss Henry, recollecting herself. "You asked me how I knew about hardened deceivers. It was like this. Within a fortnight of my being left alone in the world, I had the misfortune to meet two of them." Warming to her subject, she went on quickly, "One of them — a young gentleman who was the son of our landlord and very *gentil,* it *appeared*, made many protestations to me of an entirely legitimate passion. You understand that I was in a very difficult position at the time: I had no money. When with the utmost reluctance I made up my mind to accept his offer, he — he said that I had mistaken his meaning, and he made me a very improper proposal instead."

The Baroness clicked her tongue sympathetically, and Jasper, though privately of the opinion that any man who offered Miss Henry a *carte blanche* ought to be decorated for bravery, besides being decidedly uncritical as to the essential points to be looked for in a *chère-amie*, did likewise.

"So then," continued Miss Henry, "I decided to go on the stage, so I went to visit a friend of *Maman*'s who is a theatrical manager. He said it would be an affair of the simplest to find me a situation in which I would soon become an ornament of the Comédie-Française, and then *he* made me an improper proposal. When I said *No* he was very much put out, and ended by sending me off to a horrid little company that played only in the most undistinguished theatres in provincial towns."

"Exactly. Obviously quite unsuited to your talents," said Jasper, quick to seize the opening. "Dear Miss Henry, why don't you throw the whole thing over and accept my offer? I can promise you that there will be no proposals of any kind, proper or improper, and only think what sort of husband you will be able to nobble with that ten thousand pounds in your pocket. Baronets' granddaughters are as common as gooseberries in England, I can tell you, but young women with dowries of ten thousand pounds can command the very best on the market. Well, if not the best," he emended it, anxious to be no less than scrupulously honest lest he too be classed as a hardened deceiver, "at least a very respectable article."

Miss Henry said practically that if she had ten thousand pounds she would not need a husband, a piece of Gallic wisdom which the Baroness warmly applauded. The latter then said it was growing late if they wished to make arrangements for Miss Henry to be transformed into Giles Arcourt that evening, upon which Miss Henry replied, with something of an air of digging in her heels and laying her ears back, that she had not yet make up her mind to be Giles Arcourt.

"Flummery!" said the Baroness encouragingly. "Of course you have. Depend upon it, if you go back to Calais they will have taken offence at your leaving so suddenly and you will be obliged to compromise your virtue in order to live. I cannot in good conscience allow you to do that. Come along to my bedchamber, dear child. Jasper and I have purchased a wardrobe *de la plus soigné* for Giles Arcourt, though the boots," she observed, regarding Miss Henry's slender feet, "may perhaps be a trifle large. We shall be obliged to crop your hair, of course, but you will look charming with it worn *au coup de vent.*"

Miss Henry, succumbing to the Baroness's insistence, allowed herself to be drawn to her feet; Jasper rose and bowed; and in a matter of a few moments she was in the Baroness's room just down the hall, watching Disbrey, the Baroness's dresser, removing from the wardrobe a coat of dandy russet, a neat buff waistcoat, a cambric shirt, severely unruffled in the fashionable mode, prime doeskin pantaloons, and a pair of mirror-polished boots, the whole to be worn over discreet black silk drawers and stockings.

"Perhaps a trifle too elegant," the Baroness said, critically examining the ensemble, "for a youth in the situation in life in which you have presumably been brought up, but neither Jasper nor I could bear to think of your appearing in anything distressingly *démodé,* so we decided you were to have been much indulged by your foster-parents. You will learn the whole story of your past as you travel to Arcourt's Hall with Jasper. It is rather neat, I think. Jasper and I had a most interesting time inventing it on the way down.''

Miss Henry was looking rather mulishly at the clothing now laid out for her upon the bed. She evidently distrusted the presence of Disbrey, a dour-faced Scotswoman who had been obliged by the circumstances of her employment to spend a good deal of her life abroad, which accounted for her expression of perpetual disapproval; and she would perhaps have bolted had it not been for the fact that she found herself, in the twinkling of a bedpost, set down before a mirror, the pins ruthlessly removed from her mane of dark-coppery curls, and a pair of scissors snipping away busily about her ears.

After that, of course, it was too late to retreat. She had been used, in dressing herself for the breeches parts in which she had recently appeared, to viewing herself in a mirror wearing the powdered *ailes de pigeon* wig, with its rows of tightly rolled curls on the temples and its pigtail tied with a bow in back, that had been the favoured masculine style of an earlier generation; but now she saw herself transformed as if by the stroke of a fairy's wand into a thoroughly modern youth, her own coppery hair ruthlessly cropped in a charming and fashionable style which seemed to demand the dandy russet coat, the tight-fitting Inexpressibles, and the brilliantly polished boots.

"Excellent! Oh, ex-cel-lent!" exclaimed the Baroness, quite in raptures when she saw her at last dressed from head to foot as "Giles Arcourt." "My dear, you look heavenly; you are quite *lost* as a girl. Those lovely long straight legs — it is a positive crime to hide them in skirts. Can you swagger just a bit? I *do* like a young man to carry himself with an air!"

Miss Henry, regarding herself critically in the mirror, decided that she, too, approved of the effect. She confided to the Baroness that when her father had been alive he had permitted her to ride astride far beyond the age at which her *maman* had considered it *convenable*, and that she had often found it vexing to be obliged to confine her activities within the narrow range felt to be proper for a young lady.

"Perhaps," she conceded, "people *will* believe, after all, that I am a young man."

And to test her newly assumed masculinity she strode across the room in an Amazonian style, came to a halt before the chimney piece with legs astraddle, and dug her hands casually into her breeches pockets.

"Splendid!" said the Baroness. "Now this is what you must do. Go down the back stairs — I have had Disbrey spy out the lay of the land for you — and then go round to the front door and walk in and ask the landlord for a room for the night. It will be a splendid test to see if he recognises you, but I am quite sure that he will not. Here are your hat and portmanteau" — as Disbrey produced them, as if by sleight-of-hand, from the wardrobe. "And I expect you will need some money — "

She tossed a purse to Miss Henry, who caught it and, without examining it to see what was inside, stowed it away in her pocket.

29

"I shall have your own things packed up with mine," said the Baroness, looking with a slight shudder at the duffle cloak, the deplorable hat, and the plain round gown that Miss Henry had removed, "though I trust that when you have received your ten thousand pounds you will have no further use for them. I should make Jasper sign an agreement, if I were you. It is not that he is in the least dishonest, but I always say it is a great mistake to enter into any sort of relationship with a man without pinning him down, and it will set the whole matter on a properly businesslike footing, exactly like marriage settlements. He will be taking you to Arcourt's Hall tomorrow, as I told you, which is *quite* out of the way and completely deserted except for a pair of old servants, so that you may remain there in perfect seclusion until you have learned all about the splendid background we have invented for you. *Don't* — whatever you do — let Jasper bully you. Not that he could, I expect; I saw from the first moment that yours was a very strong character. Are there any more questions?" she then asked briskly, as if she were presiding over a meeting and had decided that it was time it came to an end.

Miss Henry looked as if there were a great many, but contented herself with asking how "Giles Arcourt's" first meeting with Mr. Jasper Carrington was to come about.

"Jasper will see to that," the Baroness said carelessly. "We rather thought he might fall into conversation with you over breakfast in the coffee-room, and be so stunned, when you disclose your name to him, that he will make the sort of scene people will remember, just in the event those tiresome lawyers come nosing about later. As for you, you have just discovered your true identity, you see, and are on your way to Arcourt's Hall to try to find your long-lost relations there. But as you are an actress, I daresay you will find no difficulty in picking up your cues."

Miss Henry, who had been an actress for a very short time indeed, felt these assurances to be rather inadequate, but nevertheless found herself, not three minutes later, standing outside the rear of the inn in her male clothing in the pouring rain, a portmanteau containing she knew not what in her hand and a purse containing she knew not how much in her pocket.

"If I had the slightest degree of sense," she told herself gloomily in French, which was the language she habitually used for thinking in, "I should depart from this place as rapidly as possible and return to France. *Vraiment, c'est incroyable!*"

But, incredible as her situation undoubtedly was, she did not, as wisdom directed, depart from the Ship Inn, but instead picked her way carefully around to the front door, where she made the kind of entrance that, had she been upon a stage, would have earned her a cordial round of applause.

THREE

Fortunately, Miss Rolande Henry was a girl who adapted quickly to new situations. When she awoke in the morning and found herself in a comfortable bed-chamber in an English inn, with an English cock crowing outside under a bright English sun, and English voices, raised in an acrimonious argument that appeared to concern fish, floating up to her from below, she did indeed blink in bewilderment for a few moments, especially when her eyes fell upon a set of un-mistakably male garments strewn about the room.

But recollection of the amazing events of the previous night returned quickly, and, after one panic-stricken moment when she could not recall the name of the young man she was at present impersonating, she found herself accepting the situation philosophically. After all, she reflected, what was to happen could not be much worse than the events of a memorable night in St. Petersburg when she and her father and mother, owing to a slight difficulty over arrears in payment for their lodgings, had been obliged to flee the city in a snowstorm in the dead of winter at the witching hour of midnight.

Had she known anything of Mr. Jasper Carrington's habits, she would have realised that it was far too early to expect to meet him when, at half-past eight, she strolled downstairs to have her breakfast in the coffee-room. She had had considerable trouble in achieving a satisfactory arrangement of the yard-long strip of starched white muslin that formed her cravat, but otherwise she believed her appearance to be beyond reproach. This presumption was strengthened when an elderly gentleman from Hertfordshire who had just returned from the Continent fell into conversation with her over a breakfast of soused herrings, buttered eggs, and toast, and appeared perfectly ready to accept her as being precisely what her clothes proclaimed her to be.

Rather flown with this success, and as Jasper had still not appeared in the coffee-room when she had finished her breakfast, she was emboldened to put her disguise to a further test by going out into the bright, gusty morning for a short walk about the town, of which she had been able to see nothing at all when she had arrived, owing to the darkness and the pouring rain. The waterfront, where sloops, brigantines, hoys, and Revenue cutters lay in the harbour under a sparkling blue sky and an exciting bustle of arrival and departure enlivened the scene, she found particularly interesting, especially since, as a young man, she was allowed to lounge about anywhere without encountering so much as a single raised eyebrow.

All at once, however, she heard a hiss behind her,

and turned about to see Jasper regarding her with an exasperated expression upon his handsome, ruggedly aristocratic face. He wore an exquisitely fitting coat of Bath superfine, pale yellow breeches, and white-topped boots; his cravat was arranged in the highly fashionable style known as the *Trône d'Amour*; and a curly-brimmed beaver crowned his crisp, fair locks. The only thing lacking to make him the dandy complete was that there was no expression of ineffable boredom on his face. Jasper found life far too interesting to be bored by it, and even when he was in a bad temper, as he was at present, his grey eyes looked alert and willing to be amused.

"What are you doing here?" he demanded of Rolande in an indignant voice. "Didn't the Baroness tell you we were to meet at breakfast in the coffee-room?"

"I have had my breakfast. I was hungry," Rolande said simply.

Jasper gazed at her severely. "That," he said, "is a very poor excuse, my girl. You can't expect to earn ten thousand pounds, you know, without making a few sacrifices along the way."

"Perhaps I could meet you at luncheon," Rolande suggested, appearing not at all put out by this rebuke. "How do you like my clothes and my hair? Do you think I look now like a boy?"

She pulled off her hat to display her coiffure. Jasper looked at her and groaned.

"What is the matter?" she asked, affronted. "I think I look very nice."

"With that — that *thing* round your neck? Do you call that a cravat?" demanded Jasper, unconsciously paraphrasing Mr. Brummell's comment on a ducal coat. "What on earth have you done to it?"

"I have never learned properly how to arrange a cravat," Rolande said with dignity. "It is not *comme il faut* for a *jeune fille bien-élevée* to know such tings."

"Well, you're not a *jeune fille bien-élevée* now; you're a boy," Jasper retorted. "And I'm not going to be seen in public with a horror like that! Come along to my bedchamber and I'll tie it properly for you."

He set off towards the inn with long strides, so that she had almost to run to keep up with him.

"But I have not met you yet!" she protested, when she had managed to get enough breath to speak. "You said we were first to fall into conversation — "

"We have fallen into conversation," Jasper said curtly. "At the harbour. I have now discovered that you are my cousin and am taking you back to Arcourt's Hall with me."

Rolande said a trifle sulkily that he seemed to change his plans in a great hurry, but secretly admired his gift for rapid improvisation. At the inn they found the Baroness scratching on the door of Jasper's bedchamber. She said she had decided not to go to Paris after all.

"I shall be certain to miss all the most interesting parts of the plot if I do," she said. "I know you have told me, dearest Jasper, that the Court is not in session now, so that nothing of importance can occur until they begin sitting again, but you *are* planning on introducing *your* Giles Arcourt to Honoria, aren't you? But you must! I have been making the most exciting plans for the meeting — *two* Giles Arcourts in one room, and Honoria trying to look as if she was having tea with the Queen while green fury darts from her eyes. Yes, I know her eyes are blue — *quite* unfair, for one always believes blue-eyed people speak the truth.''

Jasper said that she had best go to Paris because there would be no such scene; it was his fixed intention, he said, to keep Miss Henry in the strictest seclusion until the proper moment came for loosing her upon the legal profession, to his aunt Honoria's confusion.

He then sat Rolande down in a chair, stripped off the offending cravat, and replaced it with one of his own, which he deftly arranged in the style known as the Osbaldeston, as being suited, he said, to her youth and inexperience. The Baroness meanwhile directed that her luggage, which was exceedingly voluminous, be replaced in the huge travelling chariot that had brought it down to Dover the day before, instead of being placed aboard the Calais packet.

"I shall go to Brighton," she said. "It is by far the best plan, for Honoria is already there and then I shall be close at hand when things begin to happen."

Jasper repeated that nothing was going to happen, but she quite obviously did not believe him and went on making her plans, which included ousting old General Pusey from the very desirable house on the Steyne he had hired for the summer in the event that no other suitable lodgings were available.

"He still hopes to seduce me," she said superbly,

when Jasper pointed out that it was highly unlikely she would succeed in evicting the General — which, as the General was rising eighty, Jasper considered even more unlikely.

But, as he told Rolande when they were ensconced together in a hired post-chaise on their way to Buckinghamshire (the Baroness having pre-empted his own travelling chaise in which she had journeyed down from London with him), his cousin Louisa had a way of getting what she wanted in spite of all obstacles, so he dared say if she didn't put old General Pusey out she would put someone else out and come up with the sort of house that suited her.

Rolande, who had a very logical mind and had been awaiting her opportunity to pin Jasper down to a more detailed account of the scheme in which she was to take part, at this point began to cross-examine him on the matter. She was somewhat hampered, however, by the fact that, never having seen the English countryside before, she found her attention wandering frequently to objects in the Kentish landscape — a huge half-timbered manor house, looking as if it had grown like an enormous mushroom out of the earth; cherry orchards; oast-houses raising their conical profiles against a hot azure sky; the inky blue-black shadows beneath a grove of pine trees.

"It is like a dream," she said suddenly, interrupting Jasper.

"What is?" asked Jasper.

"All of this. My clothes, this country, what you are telling me of a plot to take all those millions of pounds away from you. I am not at all sure that I believe any of it. I shall probably awaken soon and find myself back in Calais again."

Jasper assured her that she would do nothing of the sort and, apparently under the impression that she was about to become difficult again and that the best way to restore her to good humour was to feed her, told the postillions to stop at the next inn they passed and ordered an enormous luncheon of Flemish soup, prawns, mushroom fritters, and calf's fry for her. She consumed it all calmly, causing Jasper to remark that it appeared to him that he would be obliged to deduct the cost of provisioning her from her ten thousand pounds, as she might otherwise double the amount before he had finished with her.

"I do not care," she said. "I know it is not *convenable* for a *jeune fille bien-élevée* to eat so much, but, as you have pointed out, I am a boy now, and boys may eat as much as they like. Besides, I have not had enough to eat since *Maman* died. That is a thing I like very much about you," she assured him. "You are a good provider."

Jasper said he had been told as much, which caused her to look at him with sudden suspicion and enquire whom he had had to provide for.

"Oh, various people, here and there," Jasper said evasively.

Rolande gave a knowledgeable shrug.

"Your personal affairs," she said rather severely, "are no concern of mine, Mr. Carrington, but I hope you will remember that ours is a strictly business relationship. I consider myself to be in your employ for the time being, exactly like your housekeeper, with whom I am sure you would not dream of entering upon a more intimate relationship."

Jasper said that when she met Mrs. Gilray at Arcourt's Hall she would realise how very right she was, was rebuked with a glance for levity, and was brought back at once, as soon as they had re-entered the post-chaise, to the subject of the missing Giles Arcourt.

"How can you be sure that that unfortunate child is really dead?" she demanded. "It seems to me very careless of his family not to have attended to bringing him back to England at once when his parents succeeded in having him taken out of France. And what became of his parents?"

Jasper explained that they had both died in France shortly after they had arranged, when war had broken out again between France and England in 1803 following the collapse of the brief Peace of Amiens, to have young Giles removed from that country to safety.

"Of course they — meaning my uncle and his wife — should never have taken him to France in the first place," Jasper said. "But my aunt, like a true Frenchwoman, insisted on haring across the Channel, as soon as peace was declared, to look up her kith and kin and see how many of them had managed to survive the rigours of the Revolution, and, being a romantic at heart as well, she also insisted on taking the offspring, so that he could see the land of his Gallic ancestors. When they were caught by the outbreak of the war and saw no prospect of being able to leave France soon, they hit on the plan of having a pair of their servants, the Dubruls, who were Swiss, take the child out of the country. The Dubruls managed to get to Vienna with him — the Arcourts were in Strasbourg when the trouble began, so an eastern escape route seemed more feasible than an attempt to go directly to England — but as soon as they arrived there *they* both came down with some sort of fever and young Giles ended up in the hands of a couple named Schmidt. And that is as far as we go. Do you know how many Schmidts there are in Vienna, Miss Henry?''

Rolande said she dared say there were a great many, but why, she asked, had these particular Schmidts not come forward to restore the child to his family, particularly if extensive enquiries had been made?

"Lord knows," said Jasper frankly. "The best theory seems to be that the child died, too, and they were afraid to come forward for fear of being held responsible for his death. On the other hand, the version my aunt Honoria has concocted to account for *her* Giles Arcourt's dramatic reappearance is that the Schmidts had unfortunately lost the documents given to them by the Dubruls, which would have proved the child's identity, and feared they might be taken up by the authorities if they made an attempt to foist him on a wealthy English family as the missing heir. At long last, however, this version runs, upon the persuasion of my aunt's solicitor, Mr. Croil, who succeeded with bulldog tenacity in ferreting them out (and if I appear to mix my metaphors it is because Croil happens to possess the more disagreeable characteristics of both those animals), they agreed to sign an affidavit as to the events of the year '03 dealing with young Giles, as well

40

as to disgorge an opal ring that my aunt Honoria swears she gave John Arcourt before he went to France. Are you following all this, Miss Henry?''

"Yes," said Rolande. "It sound very plausible."

"Of course it does," said Jasper. "My aunt Honoria is a highly ingenious woman. Also thorough. The opal ring is a master touch. Still, I do feel the history the Baroness and I have invented for you is equally recherché. *Your* Schmidts became so fond of you, after you had been entrusted to their care by the Dubruls with their dying breaths, that they hid the papers proving your identity in an old chest and brought you up as their own son. Even when you made a chance discovery of the papers a few months ago they still refused to give you up, and destroyed the papers, so that you were obliged to set out alone on a perilous and desperate search for your real family, knowing little more of your background than that you were Giles Arcourt, the son of the late John Arcourt of Arcourt's Hall in Buckinghamshire. Of course we shall make it our business to find a pair of Schmidts in Vienna who have a runaway son — fortunately, young men run away from home with really tiresome frequency, so there should be no difficulty about *that* — and, of course, knowing nothing of any Giles Arcourt, they will deny the whole affair when taxed with it, which will be no more than is expected of them by the legal gentlemen. So that will be all right."

Rolande, who had been giving this rather complicated explanation her considered attention, said after a moment that his version of the story seemed to her to be as plausible on the face of it as did Lady Prest's,

41

which appeared to gratify Jasper.

"Thank you," he said. "I think rather well of it myself. And it should give the legal gentlemen something to think of, at any rate. We may not have as many documents as Aunt Honoria, but neither has she got a Giles Arcourt who looks exactly like his mama."

Rolande expressed a curiosity to see the portrait of the lady to whom she was reported to bear such a strong resemblance, but by the time they reached Arcourt's Hall that evening it was so late that she had no particular wish to look at anything but a hot bath and a comfortable bed, both of which were presently provided her. Not, however, without a considerable amount of scurrying about on the part of the disturbed and bewildered Gilrays, who, of course, had not been given the slightest intimation that their master intended to appear on the doorstep that evening accompanied by a youth who claimed to be the missing heir to the Arcourt millions.

FOUR

To say that the Gilrays were disturbed and bewildered by the appearance of a new Giles Arcourt at Arcourt's Hall is a mild description of the state of discomposure into which they were thrown by this event. They were an elderly couple, looking, as elderly couples often do, as like each other as fourpence to a groat, and they were devoted to Jasper, whom they had known since he had been in short coats and whom they still regarded as being quite incapable of managing his own affairs, in spite of his reputation as a world-traveller and man-about-town.

Of course they were now of the opinion that his action in receiving into his house and taking to his bosom, so to speak, a youth whose very existence threatened his inheritance of eight million pounds was clear evidence of his being in dire need of someone to look after him, and they behaved towards him with anxious solicitude, at the same time giving Rolande nothing but cold words and suspicious looks.

All this, however, made no impression whatever upon Rolande, who, when the light of a fine summer morning dawned the following day, had a delightful time, after consuming a hearty breakfast, in exploring the Hall. Arcourt's Hall was a Restoration house, built of pale, luminous chalk stone with quoins and window surrounds of darker limestone; the swelling shapes of its pedimented gables were fantastically accentuated by flanking Ionic volutes, which looked as if they had been made of spun-sugar rather than of stone, and which appeared to sway and coil as they carried the pediments aloft.

Inside, the walls were hung with faded damask and gilded leather, and the floors were enlivened by the glowing colours of carpets from Persia and Turkey, though much dimmed now with dust and neglect. In the Ivory Saloon her own face looked down, from a tarnished gilt frame, upon a long, half-bare, delightfully melancholy apartment, its elegant spindly chairs and Louis XIV sofas with their silks and brocades split and worn, but still gallantly breathing of romance. The windows overlooked a large, neglected topiary garden, where a completely illogical company of beasts and birds, corkscrews, discs, balls, and giant hats had once been carefully sculpted from yew and box, but had now grown into a fantastic jumble of extremely odd yet somehow significant shapes.

It all reminded Rolande very much of the fairy tales that had been read to her when she was a child, and she felt that if the Sleeping Beauty had been English she would certainly have lived in Arcourt's Hall.

Her obvious mood of satisfaction much relieved

Jasper, who had rather feared that the Gilrays' cold looks and the dilapidation of the house might strike her unfavourably, causing her to regret her decision to play the role of Giles Arcourt. As a reward for her good behaviour he consented to permit her to ride around the estate with him on one of the three or four superannuated hacks that still lived in the silent stables under the care of a single elderly groom, though he was not anxious to allow the neighbourhood a glimpse of her.

Still, he realised that there was no hope of keeping her entirely concealed, for as soon as the news of his arrival at the Hall got about, two or three extremely curious and ingenious ladies who lived nearby would be sure to oblige their husbands to call upon him and discover what he was up to. He had already made up his mind to tell them that Rolande was the son of a Belgian friend of his who had recently died and commended him — Rolande, that is — to his care. This would account for the slight foreignness of Rolande's accent and the fact that the bereaved youth cared to take no part in the pleasures of the dinner parties or pic-nic excursions that might be offered him.

As to the resemblance between the young Belgian and the portrait in the Ivory Saloon, that could easily be coped with by taking the portrait down. Fortunately, the late Mrs. John Arcourt had lived only briefly at the Hall, and that had been so many years ago now that no one was likely to remember exactly how she had looked.

Of course, Jasper considered, he might come out and say directly that he was entertaining his cousin, Giles Arcourt, at the Hall; but that would at once subject Rolande to an intense and curious scrutiny before she had had time to familiarise herself with all the ramifications of her role, and before he himself could receive the particulars of the circumstances of the Schmidt family now being sought out for him by a Viennese friend of his. He rather thought, therefore, that his best plan for the present was to keep Rolande out of sight as much as possible and to rely upon the Belgian explanation when caught.

As luck had it, the particular ladies whose curiosity he had most feared had already removed to Worthing for the summer when he and Rolande arrived at the Hall, and he was congratulating himself, after several days had passed, upon their agreeable solitude (it was true that he and Rolande quarrelled almost hourly over everything from her continued inability to arrange a cravat to Wellington's tactics at Waterloo; but at least he was not bored) when he and Rolande, returning one morning from their daily ride, came cantering up the drive to find a short, plump, soberly attired middle-aged gentleman just alighting from a post-chaise before the front door.

"Good God! It's Birdwhistell," exclaimed Jasper, and reined in his horse, looking at Rolande in some dismay. "My solicitor," he explained hurriedly, "and what he is doing here passeth understanding. I can't tell *him* you're a Belgian; he will certainly have to see you as Giles Arcourt when we are trying to pass you off to his legal brethren. Oh, well! I shall contrive to rub through somehow, I daresay. *En avant, mon enfant!*"

He led the way on up the drive, where Mr. Birdwhistell, who had espied their approach, stood awaiting him with a beneficent smile upon his odd-looking

46

countenance. Mr. Birdwhistell had a large nose, mild blue eyes, and very little chin, and resembled a country clergyman of scholarly tastes far more than he did a London solicitor of an awe-inspiring reputation for knowing and using every sharp twist and turn of the Law that lay within the limits of honest practice.

His mild eyes now took in Rolande very thoroughly as she reined in at the foot of the steps the chestnut mare she was riding, and an expression of almost comical astonishment abruptly replaced the benevolent smile with which he had been preparing to greet Jasper.

"Dear boy!" he stammered, wrenching his eyes with difficulty, it appeared, from Rolande's face as Jasper held out his hand to him, and collecting himself in a flurry of apologies. "You must forgive me: I fear I intrude upon your bucolic pleasures." He added, with another fascinated glance at Rolande, "You will present me, I hope, to your young friend?"

"Oh," said Jasper, with as careless an air as he was able to assume, "this is my young cousin, Giles Arcourt. Giles, Mr. Birdwhistell. Why don't you take the horses round to the stables, coz?" he added, with a meaning look at Rolande, who appeared to be on the point of dismounting after her polite acknowledgement of Mr. Birdwhistell's mesmerised bow. "I daresay Birdwhistell has come upon business, and I may be closeted with him for some time."

He gave her another speaking glance and shepherded the solicitor into the house. As soon as Gilray had taken Mr. Birdwhistell's hat, Jasper threw his own hat, gloves, and riding crop upon a hall table, told Gilray to bring some sherry, and took his guest into the

Ivory Saloon. This was a tactical error, for Gilray, although ordered to do so, had not yet removed the portrait of the late Mrs. John Arcourt from the wall, and Mr. Birdwhistell at once walked — or, rather, tottered, Jasper thought — over to it and stood looking up at it.

"A most remarkable resemblance! *Most* remarkable!" he ejaculated, taking a large handkerchief from his pocket and mopping his brow with it in a distracted manner. "Dear me! I can scarcely credit it! When news was brought to me that you were entertaining a mysterious youth at the Hall who bore a striking resemblance to the late Mrs. John Arcourt, I must confess I pooh-poohed the matter. But now—" He turned to face Jasper, an almost awestruck expression upon his round countenance. "I daresay you must realise, my dear boy," he said, "in what a *very* awkward position this places her ladyship. I am referring, of course, to your aunt, Lady Prest. The young man she has brought forward as the son of her late brother is obviously — "

"An imposter?" said Jasper, who had rapidly been considering what line he should take and had come to the conclusion that if he told Mr. Birdwhistell he had accepted *his* Giles Arcourt at face value that astute solicitor would soon begin wondering why, in that case, he was hiding him at Arcourt's Hall. "Yes, naturally that has occurred to me," he said carelessly. "On the other hand, though, can we be quite certain, either, that *this* boy is the genuine article? I know he looks very much like my late aunt — "

"My dear Mr. Carrington, the resemblance is uncanny!"

Mr. Birdwhistell permitted himself to be persuaded

to a chair, and, Gilray arriving at that moment with a bottle of Oloroso, which would never have been left in the house if Jasper had known it was there, the subject of Giles Arcourt was perforce momentarily abandoned, allowing Jasper time in which to collect his somewhat disordered thoughts. He determined to go on the attack himself, and asked Mr. Birdwhistell, as soon as Gilray had left the room, who it was that had informed him of the presence of a mysterious youth at Arcourt's Hall.

Mr. Birdwhistell waved a vaguely explanatory hand. "In my profession," he said almost apologetically, "one hears such an extraordinary number of things. They float, if I may be permitted a poetic simile, like gossamer on the breeze" — by which Jasper understood him to mean that he had no intention of disclosing the source of his information. He was aware that Mr. Birdwhistell led a sort of protean existence, being a familiar and inconspicuous onlooker at the most disparate scenes, from Bow Street magistrates' courts to polite soirées given by dowagers of impeccable reputation, and that in all these places he picked up scraps of information which he stored away as industriously as a squirrel stores away nuts for the winter.

Mr. Birdwhistell, having parried Jasper's question and drawn a further red herring across his line of enquiry by commending the Oloroso, then went back to the point where they had been interrupted by Gilray's arrival and begged Jasper to tell him what grounds he might have for believing that the youth he was now entertaining at the Hall as Giles Arcourt might not be, as he had phrased it, the genuine article.

"Oh, none at all, really," said Jasper, who was not

49

anxious to cast any more doubt than was necessary upon his own candidate. "His story seems straightforward enough." He related it, and had the satisfaction of seeing that Mr. Birdwhistell apparently found it quite as plausible as Rolande had done. "All the same," he went on, "it does seem deuced odd, two Giles Arcourts turning up after all these years. One can't help thinking that there may be a third, and even a fourth, lurking somewhere about."

Mr. Birdwhistell said rather reprovingly that this scarcely seemed likely, but admitted that he had not foreseen the probability of their being obliged to cope with a second Giles Arcourt after Lady Prest had produced the first.

"It will make for a great many legal difficulties," he said, much to Jasper's gratification. "Dear me, yes, a *great* many," He looked seriously at Jasper. "Do you know, my dear Mr. Carrington," he said, placing the tips of his fingers together with precision and contemplating them as if he found their orderly arrangement of assistance in arranging his thoughts in an equally orderly fashion, "it occurs to me that we may have been remiss — indeed, exceedingly remiss — in not having pursued a more thorough investigation before this time into the circumstances of your young cousin's disappearance in Vienna. It might have prevented the most distressing and perplexing situation in which we find ourselves today — "

"But I thought a thorough investigation *had* been pursued," Jasper said, slightly surprised.

Mr. Birdwhistell, regarding the pyramided perfection of his fingers, shook his head sadly.

"Not what *I* should call thorough," he said simply. "No, no, my dear boy, not what *I* should call thorough. The point is," he went on, warming to his subject, "that no attempt has ever been made to reach these Schmidts upon their own level. You simply cannot find out the truth from the lower classes by setting officials or men of business upon them; they mistrust them, or are afraid of them, and will go to almost any lengths to avoid telling them the truth. Now I have had a small idea in the back of my mind ever since Mr. Croil informed me that he had succeeded in discovering a youth whom he believed to be the genuine Giles Arcourt — "

The disparaging manner in which he spoke Mr. Croil's name made it clear to Jasper that there was nothing Mr. Birdwhistell would like better than to put his renowned fellow-solicitor upon display as an incompetent nincompoop.

"Yes?" he said encouragingly.

"I have had a small idea," continued Mr. Birdwhistell, "that if one were to send to Vienna a person well fitted by birth and habit of mind to obtain the confidence of these people, he might succeed where more subtle minds and more powerful resources had failed. It so happens that I have such a person more or less in my employ. He is a former member of the King's German Legion, a butcher by trade before he left his homeland to go into exile here and join the battle against the Monster Bonaparte. Not a particularly clever fellow, but thorough, very thorough, and has a certain low cunning in tracking down information that may be of value —"

"Send him to Vienna, by all means!" said Jasper,

urging another glass of the Oloroso upon Mr. Birdwhistell.

He was aware that he was taking a risk in advocating this course of action, but he reflected that if a third and genuine Giles Arcourt was actually alive at present, it would be far better to learn about it now than later, when the Court might have awarded him the eight million pounds and he would then be obliged to disgorge it. Giving up a hypothetical fortune, he felt, was a good deal easier than giving up one already in one's grasp. And if Birdwhistell's man did come up with ironclad proof that the infant Giles had died years ago, Lady Prest's schemes would be thwarted, at any rate, and he, Jasper, would get the eight million pounds.

Mr. Birdwhistell looked pleased at his immediate acceptance of his suggestion about the former member of the K.G.L., and promised to see to the matter the moment he returned to London. He then expressed a desire to speak with Rolande, and Japser, who was unable to think of any valid excuse to prevent him from doing so, was greatly relieved when Gilray, sent to fetch her, returned to say that the young gentleman had been seen by the groom to walk off through the kitchen garden into the copse after bringing the horses round to the stable, and was now nowhere to be found in the house.

"A pity!" said Jasper, taking instant advantage of this information. "I expect he won't return for hours. He seems to be fond of long, solitary rambles. And no doubt your presence is urgently required in London?"

Mr. Birdwhistell said regretfully that it was, and

that only what had appeared to him the extreme delicacy of the matter had prompted him to make the journey into the country himself instead of sending one of his underlings. He urged Jasper, however, to bring his Giles Arcourt to London as soon as possible, so that he could question him exhaustively, and impressed upon him the necessity of discovering as much as he could in the meanwhile concerning the young man's former history.

"There is no need to bring him forward until we have all the cards in our hand," he said. "If he should indeed prove to be actually your uncle's son — as I fear he must be, owing to his striking resemblance to the late Mrs. John Arcourt — you will of course be obliged to relinquish all hope of inheriting the Arcourt fortune. I must say, my dear boy," he added with the affectionate familiarity stemming from an acquaintance with Jasper almost as old as that of the Gilrays, "that you are taking all this extraordinarily well. Naturally, one's family feelings must be gratified by the prospect of having restored to one a relation whom one had believed to be lost to one forever, but one's joy might well be grievously tempered by the fact that the happy discovery carries with it the loss of an immense fortune. I must congratulate you upon the equanimity — I might even say, the stoicism — with which you have received this blow of fate."

Jasper thanked him, and got him out of the house to his waiting post-chaise as quickly as possible, for fear that Rolande might unexpectedly return. She remained invisible, however, for a good hour after Mr. Birdwhistell's departure, and then came in, professing to be famished, and displaying a singed crease on the top of her shallow-crowned beaver.

"It would appear that you have poachers in your woods," she said severely. "If I were in your place, I should take immediate steps to suppress them. As you see, I might well have been their victim instead of your rabbits."

Jasper stared at the hat incredulously. "Do you mean to tell me that someone shot at you in the woods?" he demanded.

"Not at me, of course. No doubt he did not even see me. He was after your rabbits, or something of that sort."

"In broad daylight?" said Jasper, still incredulous. "There isn't much poaching that goes on around here even at night, I can tell you; old General Blough, the local magistrate, has pretty well cleared the countryside of poachers. It's his hobby; he lies awake nights thinking of new ways to bag them."

"Well, he has not bagged this one," Rolande said decisively, "as you can very well see. What did that gentleman — your solicitor, is it? — want of you? Did I do as you wished to disappear?"

"Exactly as I wished. He's a devilish deep old file, and we'd have been in the briars fast enough if you hadn't loped off before he could begin to cross-examine you. I wish to God Franz would make haste to turn up our Schmidts in Vienna, so that we could have our story complete. Birdwhistell says the news has got round that I have a mysterious youth staying here at the Hall who bears a striking resemblance to the late Mrs. John Arcourt."

He purposely dwelt no further on the incident of the poacher, not wishing to alarm Rolande with the vague suspicions it had aroused in his mind. But the coincidence of her having had a bullet singe the crown of her hat just as it appeared that the news had begun to circulate about her presence at Arcourt's Hall seemed to him too unusual to be ignored. Of course it was within the bounds of possibility that the bullet had been fired from a poacher's gun, but he remembered the Baroness's comment, on the evening he had first discussed the matter of the inheritance with her at Lady Prest's musical soirée, that one would do almost anything for eight million pounds, and his own rather flippant rejoinder, "Even murder?"

Difficult as it was to imagine murder in connexion with one's own relations, one could not but be aware that in an earlier, lustier day one's Arcourt ancestors had not been celebrated for the scrupulousness of their regard for the Commandments. A particularly ferocious forebear, in fact, who had arrived in England with the Conqueror, had been known as Walter of the Red Hand because of his unpleasant habit of eliminating his enemies personally by a dagger thrust.

Jasper made a firm resolve, therefore, not to allow Rolande out of his sight from this time forward when she left the house. He had been ready enough to involve her in a masquerade which he had considered carried no serious risk to her, but it was another matter altogether to permit her to continue in it if it might place her in a position in which her life would be in danger. Eight million pounds was eight million pounds, he thought, but he had not inherited enough of Walter of the Red

Hand's nature to consider that even eight million pounds was worth a life, though he had a disagreeable notion that his aunt Honoria, reverting to type, might perhaps be taking the opposite point of view.

FIVE

The monotony of life at Arcourt's Hall was relieved, after an additional week had passed, by the unexpected arrival of the Baroness, who had come, she said, because she was bored to death at Brighton and was quite certain that far more interesting things were taking place at Arcourt's Hall.

"When I think how young and gay we were used to be at the Pavilion, it really makes me quite melancholy," she said, "but how can one be gay when one sees Prinny, for example, grown so enormously stout that he must make use of a most elaborate mechanical contrivance even to hoist himself upon a horse? And then he *will* persist in giving those enormous dinners — one can scarcely blame him, since he has succeeded in luring Carême from France — but thirty-six *entrées*, my dear, with four soups, four *relevés de poissons,* four *grosses pièces pour les contre-flancs,* ten *assiettes volantes de fritures,* eight *grosses pièces de pâtisserie,* thirty-two *entremets,* and four *plats de rotis* — I assure you, I do not exaggerate: it fatigues one even to read the menu.''

Jasper, who was not eager to have his cousin Louisa at the Hall, feeling that her presence would inevitably lead to those social incursions he was trying his best to fend off, represented to her the extreme inadequacy of his staff to care for any further guests, and assured her that Brighton would seem a perfect paradise of dissipation to her compared with the boredom she would find at the Hall; but to no avail. The Baroness insisted upon seeing Rolande, professed herself enchanted with the strides she had made towards assuming her male character, and told Disbrey to unpack her portmanteaux.

Rolande, for her part, was quite pleased to see the Baroness, and passed a good part of the morning following her arrival in discussing with her the shortcomings of Jasper's character, regardless of whether Jasper was present or not. The Baroness, who considered that her dashing cousin received, on the whole, far too much adulation from the female sex, was delighted by the forthrightness with which Rolande pointed out his exasperating habit of being almost invariably right in any argument in which one engaged with him, his undoubtedly autocratic manners, and the unfairness of his possessing so much casual charm that one always ended by forgiving his tyrannical impositions upon one.

''I think, myself, that he should marry,'' Rolande said judiciously. ''It would do him a great deal of good. Perhaps to a lady of an overbearing disposition — ''

''God forbid!'' said Jasper feelingly. ''If I am

ever lured into parson's mousetrap, it will be by a meek female of a conformable nature, who will never say anything but *Yes* and *Amen* to me. And as for you, my girl," he went on, fixing Rolande with a severe gaze, "the best thing I can wish for you is that you will marry a man who will beat you regularly, until he has thumped some manners into you."

"That," said Rolande loftily, "will be impossible; I should never marry such a *bête farouche*. It is my intention, as soon as I have received my ten thousand pounds, to marry a man *tout à fait sympathique*, very agreeable and handsome, who will be excessively fond of me and anxious to do everything possible to please me."

"He sounds like a dead bore to me," Jasper said unsympathetically, "and I must say I pity him from the bottom of my heart. But do as you like."

He then said he would be closeted for several hours with the superannuated steward who still looked after the remaining rags and tatters of the estate, advised Rolande to keep out of sight, and once more asked the Baroness if she would not prefer to return to Brighton. The Baroness, who always enjoyed doing what other people advised her not to, said she wouldn't think of it, but confided to Rolande when he had gone that she found the country in deep summer excessively *triste*, and probably would go back to Brighton on the following day. She then floated off in a cloud of amber lace and pale yellow ribbons to write letters, having firmly declined Rolande's urgent invitation to come for a ride or at least a walk with her.

Rolande, left alone, decided to ride. She was aware

that it was strictly against Jasper's orders for her to leave the house alone, but, not being aware of his fears for her safety, she considered this merely another instance of an unreasonably dictatorial attitude upon his part and decided to ignore the prohibition.

As the day was by this time well advanced and the sun excessively warm, she found that she did not enjoy her excursion as much as she usually did; or at least this was the excuse she made to herself for not enjoying it, being quite unwilling to admit that the absence of Jasper to quarrel with might possibly be responsible for the ride's seeming so dull. But she perversely went on hacking aimlessly about the countryside until she was very hot and uncomfortable, only to prove to herself that she was perfectly happy without Jasper.

At last, however, she turned her mare's head towards Arcourt's Hall, and as both she and the mare seemed eager to reach their home destination, she was proceeding at a good canter across the narrow rustic wooden bridge that spanned a small stream winding through the park when the mare suddenly staggered and appeared to lose her footing. The next moment, before Rolande had had time to realise what was happening, the entire floor of the bridge had disappeared beneath them and she found herself precipitated into the water below.

It had rained heavily during the night, and the stream, ordinarily a placid rivulet, was bank-full and racing with water. Rolande, struggling to free herself from the terrified mare, who was thrashing about frantically in the water, fortunately found that a portion of the collapsed bridge was jutting up out of the stream nearby her and quickly seized upon it, much regretting the fact that she was not really a young man, for if she had been, it was most probable that she would have known how to swim. As it was, she could only cling grimly to her swaying timber and call out for help, though with little expectation of finding any near.

But, to her surprise and joy, she was answered almost immediately by a familiar masculine voice, and the next moment Jasper, on his big roan, came galloping down the bank towards her. He reined in his horse at the brink of the stream, and, jumping down and splashing into the water, which was merely chest-high for his six–foot–two form, caught her firmly in his arms and strode ashore. Here he dumped her without ceremony upon the ground and stood over her, the picture of unsympathetic displeasure.

"You damned little idiot!" he said furiously. "Didn't I *tell* you not to leave the house without me?"

Rolande, who was still gasping and sputtering, her clothes muddy and dripping, her hat gone and her wet hair falling into her eyes, sat up and looked at him indignantly.

"Don't you know," she exclaimed, "that I have nearly been drowned?"

"You're dashed right you've nearly been drowned, and it was entirely your own fault!" Jasper said, with equal wrath. He pulled her to her feet. "Come along. I want to get you into some dry clothes. I can't have you going off of an inflammation of the lungs."

Rolande attempted to summon up her dignity — a

somewhat difficult task, since she was aware that she resembled nothing more impressive than a half-drowned kitten.

"One does not go off of an inflammation of the lungs on a very warm day such as this," she said, and was obliged to break off to add in an anguished tone, "Oh-h! These boots! They are full of water! I cannot walk in them!"

"There's no need for you to walk," Jasper said, mounting the roan, which had obligingly not wandered off after the mare, already halfway to the stables in a wild gallop, but stood placidly cropping the lush summer grass.

He put down his hand, told Rolande to set her foot upon his boot, and pulled her up before him in the saddle. He was almost as wet as she, and they had a very damp and rapid ride to the front door of Arcourt's Hall, where he dismounted, lifted her off the horse without ceremony, saw her inside, and informed her in no uncertain tones that he wished to talk to her as soon as she had changed into dry clothes. He then, to her astonishment, went out again, mounted the roan, and rode away.

Rolande went upstairs and removed her wet clothing, feeling a good deal discomposed by the whole incident, but perhaps less by the accident itself than by Jasper's extraordinary reaction to it. When she had dressed herself again in dry clothes, she went downstairs and found the Baroness in the little morning-room at the back of the house, reading a novel. While she was telling her what had happened, Jasper came in again.

"Well," he said, with an air of what seemed to Rolande satisfaction, though of a rather grim sort, "it's as I thought. The support has been sawed through."

Rolande and the Baroness gazed at him in astonishment. He presented, it was true, a very odd appearance, sartorially perfect from the chest up, with his snowy cravat arranged *à la Sentimentale* and his crisp, fair hair impeccable, while below that point he was as wet and mud-stained as it was possible for a human being to be. But it was his words, rather than his appearance, that had shocked his audience.

"What on earth do you mean?" the Baroness demanded. "Sawed through? Do you mean someone intentionally tampered with the bridge? But why — ?"

"For the same reason that a 'poacher's' stray bullet went through Miss Henry's hat when she was walking through the woods a few days ago," Jasper said curtly. He looked with disfavour at the elegant little straw-coloured satin-covered chairs and sofas. "I can't sit down here," he said, "so I'll say what I have to say and make it brief. Your masquerade, Miss Henry, is over. It would be very pleasant indeed for me to inherit eight million pounds, but not quite pleasant enough to see someone killed to bring it about. Shall we say, perhaps, five hundred pounds for your services to date, and you may forget all about Giles Arcourt and go back to being Miss Henry again — "

"But she *can't* do that, dearest Jasper," the Baroness immediately interposed. "*Not* if you are right in thinking — as I presume you *are* thinking — that Honoria has completely lost all her moral sense (not that I consider she ever really had any), and is willing to suborn murder to gain her ends. Of course she has the perfect tool for her purpose: I have always said that that man Croil is utterly unscrupulous. But if she has found out about *your* Giles Arcourt," she continued, "as I daresay she has, since you tell me that Birdwhistell and others have heard rumours of him, and if she is determined to put him out of the way, she will certainly not be deterred if your Giles Arcourt merely disguises himself (as it will appear to her) as a young woman and leaves Arcourt's Hall. In fact, it is *my* opinion," said the Baroness, looking at him severely, "that if you send Rolande away in that manner, *quite* unprotected, you will be doing no better than sending her to her death."

For once, Jasper looked non-plussed. "But what the devil am I to do with her, then?" he demanded. "Croil can always find someone else to employ in contriving these 'accidents,' even if his first attempts have failed. I simply can't go on having her here; it's far too dangerous, unless I keep her under lock and key. You saw what happened today, after I had strictly warned her not to go out alone."

"But you did not tell me why I should not go," Rolande protested. "Of course I should not have gone if I had known someone was trying to kill me. *En verité*, do you think it is true that they are?"

"*En verité*, I do," said Jasper. He looked at the Baroness. "See here," he said suddenly, "I think I've thought of something. Why don't you go back to Brighton tomorrow, Louisa, and take Miss Henry with you as your abigail? If she wears Disbrey's clothes and acts the part, no one observing from a distance will know the difference. They are very much of a height."

"An excellent idea!" said the Baroness cordially. "She will be *quite* safe with me." And she added dramatically, in the deep, thrilling tones that had made her a great asset in amateur theatricals in country houses all over England, "They will have to kill me first to kill her."

"But what am I to do when I arrive in Brighton?" Rolande objected, somewhat unfairly, Jasper and the Baroness felt, as they were both feeling rather clever over their plan. "I cannot go on forever being the maid of *Madame la Baronne*. Disbrey would not like it. She is already very disapproving of me, I think," she added gloomily.

The Baroness said encouragingly that that did not matter, because Disbrey disapproved of everyone, and assured her that she and Jasper would think of something, once they were safely in Brighton.

Rolande, however, did not look encouraged. "I think, *moi*, that you are making a great to-do over nothing and I should continue being Giles Arcourt," she said obstinately to Jasper. "How do you know, for example, that it was not *you* the person who sawed through the supports of the bridge wished to kill?"

"Because he saw you riding alone over the bridge and knew you must return that way," Jasper retorted. "And by what I am able to gather, from the length of time you were away from the house, he must have had ample opportunity to do his nefarious work. No, you are going off to Brighton, my girl, and there's an end to it. I could feel my hair turning white in a single night, or rather afternoon, like the fellow's in Byron's poem, while I went haring after you as fast as I could go, and when I heard you shrieking for help I made up my mind that the only thing to do was to get rid of you in my own way before someone else did it in his."

"I did not shriek," Rolande said coldly. "I merely called for help, as any sensible person would have done under the circumstances."

Jasper said that it had sounded like shrieking to him, and went off to change out of his wet clothes.

"He is a very annoying and entirely insupportable person," Rolande said stormily to the Baroness when they were alone together again. "It is a great pity, I think, that he came and rescued me. No doubt I should have done very well by myself if I had had a few moments to think of a plan, and then he would have known nothing about my having fallen into the water and would not wish to send me away in this stupid manner."

The Baroness, who was an expert in the matter of affairs of the heart, looked at her rather sharply, but said nothing, reflecting that, after all, since the masquerade of Giles Arcourt was about to end and Miss Henry would soon be quite out of Jasper's orbit, there was no point in warning her that it would do her not the slightest degree of good, and perhaps a great deal of harm, to fall in love with him.

SIX

On the following morning at dawn Disbrey, still rigid with indignation after putting up a strong but unsuccessful battle against her mistress's orders, was smuggled out of Arcourt's Hall on the floor of a farm cart driven by the elderly groom and conveyed to a village some ten miles distant, where she was to take a coach for London and thence to Brighton. A few hours later Rolande, no longer presenting the appearance of a slim youth, but wearing a prim, respectable grey gown and a close bonnet and looking the very picture of a proper lady's maid, followed the Baroness out the front door to the latter's waiting travelling-chaise, and in a few moments was whirled away down the drive towards the lodge gates and the post-road.

It was a lovely morning in high summer, with the scent of the big, purple-headed thistles already heavy in the still, sunny air and the hedgerows bright with yellow mullein and tansy; and Rolande, who had become very fond of Arcourt's Hall and its environs during her stay there, sat looking out the window of the chaise in rebellious silence, thinking disagreeable thoughts about Calais and the various unpleasantnesses connected with life in a third-rate provincial theatrical company there.

Having an enterprising nature, however, she did not long remain immersed in these gloomy reflections, but set herself to the task of persuading the Baroness that Jasper's concern over the incidents of the bridge and the poacher's bullet was much exaggerated, and that it would no doubt be perfectly safe if she were to resume her role as Giles Arcourt at some less isolated location than Arcourt's Hall.

"If I am with you, it will be impossible for anyone to try to kill me, even if they wish to, which I do not believe," she urged. "And what a pity if Mr. Carrington is obliged to be cheated out of eight million pounds by *ces scélérats*!"

The Baroness, always an upholder of the privileges of rank, said she must not call a viscountess a *scélérat*, even one who had tried to have her murdered, but professed herself to be much of the same opinion that Rolande had expressed.

"It is too bad that you didn't make Jasper sign an agreement, as I advised you," she said. "*That* would have bound him to carry out the affair to the end. But it is quite fruitless to repine over that now; the two of us will simply have to think of a plan. It is no good expecting Jasper to think of one, since he has taken this idea into his head that you must disappear, though I will say that he is quite the best person I know at that sort of thing. But if he is determined to be unco-operative, we shall be obliged to manage this alone. It is perfectly maddening to think of Honoria's succeeding in getting all his money, and I am sure I, for one, am willing to do anything I can to prevent it.''

The upshot of this conversation was that discussion of a great many complicated schemes beguiled the hours of the journey, and as both ladies were possessed of vivid imaginations and few inhibitions, a series of plots that would have been greeted with enthusiastic applause if they had been acted out upon the boards of a theatre specialising in the melodramatic were unfolded, each being eventually discovered, however, to be regrettably lacking in practicality.

"Never mind; I am sure we shall soon hit upon something that will be just the thing,'' the Baroness said, as the chaise stopped at last before the large, very desirable bow-fronted red-brick mansion on the Steyne that she had managed, true to Jasper's prediction, to hire for the summer.

Rolande, whose experience of seaside resorts, and especially of such highly fashionable ones as Brighton, was extremely limited, was delighted with the brief glimpses she had obtained of the town as they drove into it just at sunset, and secretly hoped that, whatever plan for her immediate future the Baroness might eventually fix upon, it would involve her remaining in Brighton. Still, it was not very probable, she thought regretfully, that, even if it did, it would permit her to enjoy the diversions promised by the sea-front, the splendid public buildings, and the inviting shops.

The next morning Disbrey, still almost speechless with awful disapproval over the indignities she had been obliged to suffer in her journey from Arcourt's Hall, was the first person to enter Rolande's bedchamber. She informed her that the Baroness, who had awakened at what was, for her, an extraordinarily early hour, wished to see her in her dressing-room as soon as Rolande had had her morning chocolate. Rolande, suddenly seized with the alarming idea that the Baroness, having slept on all their plans and realised the futility of each of them, had decided to send her away immediately, refused the chocolate and, thrusting her arms into one of the Baroness's exotic dressing-gowns, which had been lent her for the night, flew off to her hostess's apartments to try to persuade her not to do so.

She found the Baroness in a charming boudoir, reclining upon a chaise longue in a flounced and frilled robe of rose-pink gauze, wearing her famous black diamonds and surrounded by an extraordinary melange of perfumes, flowers, books, baubles and seals of various kinds, lace-covered cushions, and writing materials. The morning sunlight filtered in becomingly through the *clair-obscur* of rose-coloured curtains.

"Oh, here you are, my dear!" she cried, as Rolande came in. "How quick you have been, and I am so very glad, for I am simply bursting to tell you my idea! It came to me in the night, and I almost waked you up to tell you about it. But do sit down."

Rolande, quite certain now that she was being sent away, perched herself miserably upon a footstool and waited.

"The thing is, you see," the Baroness went on at once, not appearing to notice her tragical face, "that we have neglected what *ought* to have been our very first consideration, and that is finding a suitable disguise for you. You *do* see — don't you? — that wherever you are to go, you must look quite, quite different from the way you looked as Giles Arcourt. A change of sex is simply not enough; it is too easy to exchange breeches for petticoats. And then you have that very unusual dark-copper hair, which anyone who had ever seen would recognise, and it is cut so short now that one couldn't arrange it properly even in the most extreme mode. So I have decided to transform you into a Hungarian.''

"Into a *what*?" said Roland, looking — and feeling — more than a little dazed.

"A Hungarian," repeated the Baroness, who appeared to be quite enamoured of her idea, and full of enthusiasm. "One with Tartar blood and those intriguing, slightly slanted eyes. I believe I had the idea from your eyebrows: they *are* quite dark, and lift a trifle at the ends, and one could raise them even more. The most marvellous things can be done with *maquillage*, you know: you would not believe how clever Disbrey is at it! She always keeps me looking at least ten years younger than my age. And then, by the luckiest chance, you see, I have never given up wigs; I grew up in the era when everyone wore them, and it has always seemed to me the greatest folly not to avail oneself of their convenience. I have several — all jet-black, of course" (the Baroness prided herself upon her raven's wing hair, which really required no recourse to art to keep it so), "and one with such a mass of hair that one can sit on it. And I shall have Disbrey dress it most elaborately: anything more unlike that boyish crop you are wearing now it will be impossible to imagine. No one, I am sure, will have the least inkling that you have

ever been Giles Arcourt when she has done with you.
Well — what are you waiting for?'' she enquired impatiently, as Rolande continued to sit gazing at her with a rather stunned expression upon her face. ''Do go off and let Disbrey see what she can do with you!''

Rolande, understandably somewhat confused by the extraordinarily rapid changes in her state that had her, in the space of little more than four-and-twenty hours, cast in the roles of a youth, an abigail, and a Hungarian lady with Tartar blood in her veins, returned obediently to her bedchamber, where she found that Disbrey had already laid out upon the dressing-table a complicated array of rouge-pots, creams, and various other exotic-looking cosmetics. She was at once set down before the mirror, and in a remarkably short time saw ''Giles Arcourt's'' fresh, clear skin overlaid with a camellia pallor, the blue eyes mysteriously emphasised with darkened lashes and a winged lift to the black brows that gave them a slightly almond-shaped appearance, and the determined, rebellious mouth made fuller, riper, more lusciously crimson.

She was then arrayed in one of the Baroness's gowns, an elegant promenade dress of claret-coloured craped muslin with Spanish lapels, and the masses of jet-black hair to which the Baroness had referred were piled high upon her head in a complicated coronet, from which curling tendrils escaped over the ears with a maddeningly coquettish effect.

When all had been completed, Disbrey, with an expression of dour satisfaction upon her face, invited Rolande to survey the results in a tall cheval glass that stood in the room.

"*Mon Dieu! Est-ce moi?*" Rolande exclaimed in disbelief, looking at the elegant, exotic lady of fashion confronting her in the glass. She assumed a bored, haughty pose, half-closing those faintly slanting eyes with provocative effect. "Disbrey, you are a magician!" she declared, enchanted. "I must go and show the Baroness at once!"

But the Baroness was no longer in her boudoir, so Rolande ran off down the stairs, and, composing herself once more to be the *ennuyée* lady of fashion she had faced in the cheval glass, walked into the drawing room — too late to see that her hostess was not alone there. She was, in fact, sitting in conversation with a pair of callers, one a very small, regally erect lady of mature years, with a sweet, cold face, wearing a fashionable purple-bloom gown, and the other a much younger Beauty in blue, the colour of her frock intensifying the deep colour of her meltingly azure eyes. Both regarded her with interest as she walked into the room.

If it had been possible, Roland would have left the drawing room as unceremoniously as she had entered it, for she saw at once, from the momentary expression of horror that crossed the Baroness's face, that she had made a major *gaffe* by appearing there at that precise moment. Retreat, however, was impossible. Fortunately, the Baroness had not spent a quarter century in diplomatic circles all over the globe for nothing, and, recovering herself with extreme rapidity, was able to show her callers a demeanour of apparently unruffled calm when their eyes turned questioningly from Rolande to her.

"My dear Countess," she said at once, addressing

Rolande, "how *very* glad I am that you have come down! Here are two ladies whose acquaintance I am sure you will be most happy to make — my cousin, Lady Prest, and her niece, Mrs. Falkirk. The Countess Móra," she went on, completing the introduction with the most casual air in the world, not in the least as if she had just bestowed upon Rolande a name that the latter had never heard before. As the ladies exchanged greetings, the Baroness added explanatorily (Rolande with an almost automatic continuation of the blasé manner she had assumed upon entering the room), "The Countess, you see, has been kind enough to honour me by becoming my guest. This is her first visit to England and it is a strictly private one, though she has, of course, travelled extensively on the Continent. I am sure you will understand when I tell you that she has the greatest desire to live very quietly while she is in England, and to be known here only as the Countess Móra."

With this baldly outrageous hint, delivered in such a tone that her audience could not fail to catch her meaning, that the "Countess Móra" was actually a personage of exalted connexions who preferred to remain incognito during her visit to a foreign country, she leaned comfortably against the scrolled back of the satinwood sofa on which she was sitting and blandly awaited events.

Of course Rolande, whose head was whirling not only because of her sudden elevation in rank, but also because of her knowledge that she was actually in the presence of the sinister Lady Prest, whose machinations

74

might cost Jasper eight million pounds and might also, under less propitious circumstances, have cost her own life, at once realised that it was imperative for her to give a superlative performance in the role into which she had so unexpectedly been thrust. She sat down with an air of aloof calm, called up in her mind the accent of a Hungarian lady of charm and rank who had hotly pursued the dashing Major Henry at a time when the Henry ménage had been briefly located in Buda a few years before, and responded with an air of not quite condescending boredom to the attempts of Mrs. Falkirk to carry on a polite conversation with her.

Meanwhile, Lady Prest, who with her usual initiative had managed during the flurry of the introductions to waft herself over to a seat on the sofa beside the Baroness, had begun a rapid *sotto voce* conversation of her own with her.

"Dear Louisa," she said, "how enterprising of you to come up with such a plum to enliven this very dull season! But who *is* she?"

The Baroness shrugged, giving her a dramatically conspiratorial glance out of her bright, beady dark eyes.

"Ah, you see, I am pledged to the strictest confidence!" she said. "Only to you, dear Honoria, will I reveal that her mother — a beautiful creature, but, alas, with the saddest of histories! — was once my dearest friend. Love, Honoria, can be, as you know, the curse of our sex, especially when it falls to our lot to fix our affections where the beloved object has higher obligations — "

"A morganatic marriage?" Lady Prest, always

practical, brought these romantic hints into prosaic focus by enquiring; but the Baroness was not to be so easily drawn into the open.

"No, no — my lips are sealed," she proclaimed. "While she is with me, she will be to me, as to the world, the Countess Móra. I shall say no more. I am very happy, for her mother's sake, to have her with me in England, and I shall do my utmost to see to it that her holiday here is marred by no unseemly notoriety."

She then, being quite aware that Rolande might be experiencing considerable difficulty in keeping up a conversation in the character of a young lady of whom she knew no more than her name, turned to Peggy Falkirk, and enquired if she planned to attend the ball at the Castle Inn Assembly Rooms that evening.

"Oh, yes," said Peggy, smiling the ready, mild smile that had once caused Jasper to characterise her as the most agreeable woman in England. "Aunt thinks it will amuse Giles. He is turning into the most precocious beau since we have come to Brighton, you know; he has adonised himself to the top of fashion, and flirts with all the pretty women as if he were at least a dozen years older than his actual age." She added, in polite explanation, to Rolande, "I am speaking of my aunt's young nephew, Giles Arcourt, who has had a most romantic history and has only recently returned to England after having been reared abroad. He is no more than seventeen, and completely inexperienced, but he is a very pretty boy, with great expectations, and I rather fancy his head is being turned ever so little by all the attention he is receiving from the female sex."

The Baroness said robustly that he had best enjoy it

while he could, since it was perfectly apparent that the boy was an imposter and would be unmasked as such before many more weeks had passed.

"Oh, do you think so?" said Lady Prest sweetly. "Perhaps you are in Jasper's confidence, then. One hears he is harbouring a youth bearing a vague resemblance to my poor brother John's wife at the Hall. So enterprising of dear Jasper, but one *does* feel that resemblance counts for so little in the Law."

Rolande, who had an uncomfortable feeling that Lady Prest, if encouraged to dwell upon the subject, might discern a vague resemblance between the Countess Móra and the late Mrs. John Arcourt as well, here took advantage of the privilege of her rank by assuming an attitude of extreme lack of interest and turning the subject by asking Peggy Falkirk if she found public balls amusing.

"To me, you understand, they are quite unknown," she said. "In my position, one does not — " She waved her hand in a languid gesture of resignation. "But," she went on, as Peggy appeared about to speak, "I can see no reason why, since I am now in England, where matters are arranged quite differently, I believe — is it not true that the Regent himself sometimes condescends to appear at these balls? — I may not discover for myself what they are like. Is it not so, Madame?" she appealed to the Baroness, who, quite enchanted by her audacity, restrained herself with difficulty from applauding and agreed that indeed it was.

It had, in fact, occurred to her as soon as Rolande had walked into the room, thus making her meeting with Lady Prest inevitable, that they had now been presented with the perfect solution as to what to do with her during the interval that must elapse before she could properly be brought forward as Giles Arcourt. Not even Lady Prest, the Baroness believed, with her genius for the bold, unscrupulous stroke, would guess that the youth she was seeking with mayhem in her heart was residing openly in Brighton under her very nose. Therefore Rolande must obviously remain the Countess Móra and, as such, she, the Baroness, would be able to keep her constantly under her eye, thus being in the best possible position to prevent any harm being done to her.

The visit wound to an amicable conclusion, with all the parties agreeing to meet again at the Castle Inn Assembly Rooms that evening, and the moment the door had closed behind the callers Rolande and the Baroness flew into each other's arms in enthusiastic mutual congratulation.

"My dear, you were perfectly *splendid*!" exclaimed the Baroness.

"Oh, but it was *your* idea, Madame!" Rolande insisted.

"I *don't* know how I was clever enough to think of it! I assure you, when I saw you walk into the room I was ready to sink! Then it all came to me in a flash, the way they say one's entire life does when one is drowning, and I simply opened my mouth and said it, as if I had known it all along. And I must say you went along with it beautifully! I expect you must actually be a far better actress than I had suspected."

"Yes, I thought myself that it went very well," Rolande said modestly. "Fortunately, I happen to have had an excellent opportunity to observe a lady of that type. She was always excessively *fatigué*e with life, but very energetic in getting anything she wanted for herself. How did you like my accent?''

''Perfect! One of those unusual ones — French, but with something a trifle too robust in the r's and overemphasised in the vowels — that one finds it so difficult to place. Which is exactly as it should be, as it gives everyone a great deal of freedom of conjecture about your national origin. I think, myself, that the concensus will probably be that you are the daughter of the ruler of one of those multitudinous little German states by a Hungarian lady of high degree — it is simply impossible, you know, for anyone to remember precisely what the social situation is in Stolberg, Württemberg, Hesse-Darmstadt, Brunswick-Wolfen-büttel, et cetera, et cetera. But I myself shall take care to drop a few hints about something rather more interesting. A Russian connexion, I should think, would do you a great deal more good, and then they are so far away that it is always difficult to know exactly what they have been up to.''

The two ladies then went upstairs to plan Rolande's dress for the ball that evening. Fortunately, the Baroness dressed very youthfully for her years and squandered on clothes so much of the enormous fortune left her by the late Baron that there was no difficulty in finding something for the Countess Móra to wear which would not be recognised as belonging to her hostess. They settled at last upon a *robe de Levantine* of pale sapphire satin to be worn with azure-striped satin slippers, long gloves, a sapphire necklace, and a spray of curled ostrich plumes dyed the same sapphire blue to be set in the masses of black hair conferred on her by the wig.

It did not occur to either of them to wonder how Jasper would take this new and daring venture they were engaged in. But if it had, and had they been assured of his disapproval, they would probably not have been deterred in the least from going on with it.

SEVEN

The Baroness and the "Countess Móra," escorted by old General Pusey, who, having given up his house to the Baroness, had been accorded his reward in permission to gallant them to the ball, arrived at the Assembly Rooms at a fashionably late hour that evening. Most of the members of the *haut ton* who were spending the summer in Brighton were already gathered in the elegant rooms designed by John Crunden when the two ladies walked in, and it was obvious, from the interested glances directed at them, that word of the mysterious visitor the Baroness was entertaining in her house on the Steyne had already begun to circulate.

Rolande, who was looking most alluring in her borrowed finery and was acting to the hilt her part as a regal lady of fashion, allowed several gentlemen, who were clamouring for the privilege, to be presented to her, but rejected, with an indifferent shrug of the shoulders, all their respectful requests to be permitted to lead her onto the floor. She said she had not yet made up her mind whether or not she would dance.

"It is very warm — is it not so?" she said in the deliciously deliberate accent she had assumed, and waved her fan, an exquisite Cabriolet with ivory sticks and guards, gently before her face. A trio of gentlemen instantly sped off to procure a glass of iced lemonade for her.

This, to a young lady with an exceedingly limited experience of male adulation, was heady stuff, and the Baroness began to wonder, with her first tiny pang of doubt, whether she had been so very wise, after all, in allowing her young guest to embark upon this new masquerade.

"Heaven knows, she has *come out* amazingly in that gown," she thought. "She has just the kind of tall, slender, supple figure that is most admired now; her skin is excellent, her shoulders magnificent, and the effect of those eyes quite devastating. Someone is bound to fall in love with her, and if *she* falls in love with him in return, we shall all find ourselves in the basket. Fortunately, she appears to hold the entire male sex in a certain scorn, but all the same I do wish Jasper were here! He seems to be able to control her at least to some extent."

Had she but known it, Jasper, who had arrived in Brighton only half an hour before and had gone at once to call upon her at her house on the Steyne, where he had had a brief conversation with Disbrey, was at that very moment in a bedchamber of the Old Ship Inn, changing out of boots and breeches into the knee-smalls, silk stockings, and pumps that were requisite for an appearance in the Castle Inn Assembly Rooms. There was, had she also but known it, a curse on the vagaries of womankind on his lips and the rooted intention in his mind of dragging the "Countess Móra" away from the ball by the scruff of her neck, if necessary.

Meanwhile, Rolande, sipping iced lemonade and enjoying to the utmost the unwonted experience of having at least six young men buzzing round the small gilt sofa on which she sat, while ladies ranging in rank from admirals' wives to peeresses quietly manoeuvred themselves, as if by accident, into positions in which the Baroness was obliged to introduce them to her, had caught sight of Lady Prest and Mrs. Falkirk across the room. They were in company with a very young, very fair youth wearing a coat with a collar of such inordinate height, and a cravat so elaborately arranged, that it appeared impossible for him to look anywhere but straight before him. The coat was further embellished with a great deal of padding in the shoulders and a set of large silver basket-work buttons, and the blond locks above it had been carefully arranged in curls, in the slightly effeminate style known as *à la cherubim*.

Without a doubt, Lady Prest's Giles Arcourt, Rolande thought; she would have to think of him by that name, she felt, since she had no notion what his real one might be. And so great was her curiosity to discover what sort of interpretation her rival imposter was bringing to the role she herself had recently been essaying that she gestured negligently, summoning one of her attendant swains, and enquired of him, "Who is that pretty boy with Lady Prest? Is it the nephew, perhaps, who has, one hears, a history of the most romantic?''

''Oh yes, Madame — young Arcourt,'' said the swain, a young viscount name Hoult. He looked jealously across the ballroom at Giles. ''Stands to inherit eight million pounds, I believe. A bit pudding-faced, though, and not at all up to the rig — well, I mean to say, only *look* at that coat — ''

''I should like to speak with him, all the same, whether he has a face like a pudding or not,'' Rolande said with decision. ''Perhaps you will bring him to me? I hear he has a very interesting story to tell.''

The jealous Lord Hoult went off, and the Baroness, who had been hovering about Rolande like a mother hen who has seen one of her chicks suddenly transformed into a swan and is in the greatest uncertainty as to how it intends to conduct itself in this new guise, frowned portentously at her and warningly shook her head. Rolande ignored her, merely flirting her fan in a manner that obviously indicated an attitude of obstinacy. The Baroness, wishing more and more for Jasper's presence, cast her eyes heavenward and hoped for the best while expecting the worst.

In a few moments young Lord Hoult returned with Giles Arcourt, who was looking quite as lumpish as he had when the Baroness had met him at Lady Prest's musical soirée, but had obviously gained a good deal of assurance since that time. He made his bow to Rolande, exuding the subtle fragrance of Steek's lavender water, and when she invited him to sit beside her, displacing for the purpose one of her other admirers, smirked at her in a way that left not the least doubt in her mind that he could not possibly be Jasper's cousin. It was quite within the bounds of possibility, she was ready to admit, that Jasper's relations might be guilty of murder, grand larceny, and the various other crimes that people of large passions and few inhibitions occasionally commit; but that he could be nearly connected with anyone quite so self-satisfied and obnoxiously underbred as the smug youth seated beside her she refused to believe.

She turned her most charmingly languid smile upon him.

"So," she said, "you are the young man who has so romantically been restored to the bosom" — she caught herself up and looked enquiringly at the Baroness. "It is *comme il faut* that I say in English, the *bosom* of his family, Madame?" she appealed to her.

"Quite *comme il faut*," the Baroness assured her sweetly, looking daggers at her out of her bright black eyes.

Rolande again completely ignored her.

"Now I wish," she went on, to the obviously fascinated Giles, "that you will tell me all about yourself. We shall speak in German, so that we shall be more comfortable — it was in Vienna, I believe, that you were reared? These gentlemen, I am sure, will be quite uninterested in a conversation they do not comprehend, and so will go away — "

She looked expectantly at her admirers, who gazed at each other in despair, none of them knowing a word of German, and melted away into the throng about them.

Not so harebrained, after all, thought the Baroness

approvingly, quite reversing her opinion of Rolande's tactics. *Heaven knows what damaging admissions she may be able to extract from him while they are babbling away in his native tongue. I believe I have been underestimating that girl.*

And she abandoned her watch over the Countess Móra and walked off, to be accosted at once by her cousin Honoria's son, young Lord Prest, who requested an introduction to the Countess.

"My dear Geraint, don't you see that she is sitting with your *cousin Giles*?" the Baroness enquired. "Why don't you ask *him* to present you?"

Geraint shrugged his shoulders, a slight, uncomfortable smile on his handsome dark face.

"Well, you know, Cousin Louisa," he said, "I am finding that I have quite enough of Giles in the family circle without seeking him out in public places as well. I know I oughtn't to carp — I realise very well that he has had few advantages — but he is turning into the most insufferable young cawker it has ever been my misfortune to know!"

"Something very brummish about him, certainly," agreed the Baroness, regarding Giles, who, quite unconscious of the disfavour in which he was being held, went on talking volubly to Rolande. "Have you ever considered, dear boy, that he may be taking you all in?"

"Taking us in? Taking in Croil and my mama?" Geraint laughed. "Good Lord, no, how could he? — a halfling like that? He has more hair than wit, I can tell you; Croil would have him turned inside out in five minutes if he was trying to run any sort of rig." He dismissed the subject of Giles Arcourt and returned to that of the Countess. "Peggy says she's by way of being a mystery; is she?" he enquired. "A Tartar princess, or something of the sort? The wildest rumours are beginning to circulate. The top one is that she is actually the Regent's daughter by a Hungarian countess, and that now that the Princess Charlotte is married and an heir to the throne safely on the way, he intends to receive her in England — "

"Good heavens, is that what they are saying?" exclaimed the Baroness, trying not to look gratified, for she had dropped a vague hint to this effect in the ear of a peeress well known for her desire to be first with the latest *on-dit* or crim. con. story, and could not but be pleased with the result. "People *do* think of the most extraordinary things!" she said.

"It isn't true, then?"

The Baroness waved an admonitory finger at him. "Dear boy, as I told your mama, I am pledged to strictest secrecy!" she said, and walked off, promising to present him to the Countess later in the evening, when she should have finished her conversation with Giles Arcourt. She was not at all sure that all these presentations and conversations with the persons most nearly concerned with the Arcourt affair were wise, but she consoled herself with the thought that the less she tried to hide the Countess from Lady Prest, the less Lady Prest would think she had to hide.

The next person her eyes fell upon was Jasper, who had just walked into the room and stood looking about him with such a threatening expression upon his face that a man named Farquharson, with whom he had had a slight disagreement before leaving London, at once became convinced that he was looking for him to call him out and departed from the room with speed and dismay, collecting his belongings at the Old Ship Inn and never stopping until he had arrived in London.

The Baroness, a woman of great courage but feeling some trepidation upon her own part, took the bull by the horns and walked straight up to Jasper.

"So agreeable to see you again, dearest Jasper!" she said. "So you have decided to leave Arcourt's Hall! I hope you had a pleasant journey?"

Jasper turned his thundercloud face upon her.

"Stop trying to flummery me, Louisa!" he said accusingly. "I know what you've been up to."

"Oh!" said the Baroness, slightly taken aback. "You mean the 'Countess Móra' affair, I expect. Have you found out about that already? Well, I couldn't help it. Come along and I shall tell you about it. We can't talk properly here."

"I have no intention of going anywhere without that girl," Jasper said grimly. 'I came here to take her away. Where is she?"

"Oh!" said the Baroness again, but this time with a rather intrigued note in her voice. "Don't you see her?"

She watched him as his eyes went quickly around the room. He frowned, and made the circuit again, more slowly. She saw that his glance went straight over the Countess Móra and passed on. To be sure, she thought, Rolande was across the room from them, but still it was something of a triumph.

"I shan't tell you where she is," she announced,

"unless you promise not to make a scene. That, of course, would be fatal."

"I have no intention of making a scene," said Jasper, between his teeth. "I shall merely tell her very firmly that she is to leave."

"She won't go."

"What!"

"It's no good your saying *What*! like that, dearest Jasper. She won't go," repeated the Baroness, who was rather enjoying herself. She had no objection to seeing Jasper taken down a peg, and was looking forward to observing his face when he recognised the Countess Móra. "She is having a great success," she said, "and is enjoying herself tremendously, and, besides, there is not the least danger of anyone's connecting her with Giles Arcourt. Geraint tells me that his set are saying she is a Tartar princess, or perhaps Prinny's daughter by a Hungarian lady of high degree — though Prinny, as you well know, has always been *notoriously* insular in his *affaires*. But young people are so badly educated these days."

"And what do you think happens when Prinny himself hears this interesting *on-dit*," Jasper asked, "and perhaps expresses a desire to meet the young lady who is rumoured to be so nearly related to him?"

"Oh, that does not trouble me in the least!" the Baroness said largely. "After all, he is quite capable, if he sees her and takes a fancy to her, of convincing himself that the story is entirely based on fact and he really did have an *affaire* with a luscious Hungarian — you know he is apt to tell the most amazing tales of his personal feats of valour during the war, which I am quite sure he believes, though no one else does. But you had best come along and allow me to present you to the Countess Móra, since you seem quite unable to find her for yourself," she continued. "And do remember, pray, that you have never seen her before in your life."

She led the way around the floor, skirting the dancers, to the sofa on which Rolande was still seated. It had now been vacated by Giles Arcourt, and his place had been taken by half a dozen other young men. Two of them were sitting on the floor at her feet, Turkish fashion.

When Jasper and the Baroness were no more than six feet from the sofa Jasper stopped and stared at the exquisite Countess in her pale sapphire-blue gown, with sapphires trembling in her ears and in the dusky masses of her jet-black hair.

"What — !" he ejaculated. "You don't mean that *that —* ?"

"Yes, I do," said the Baroness, delighted. "Doesn't she look lovely? And *so* exotic! I should never have believed Disbrey could work such a miracle with her. She is really a very handsome young woman, you know, only one has never been able to see it properly because of her wearing such deplorable clothes and then having to be disguised as a boy."

Jasper, still looking stunned, allowed himself to be led up to the Countess and presented to her. He had the satisfaction of observing that her eyes flew up to meet his, as he approached, with a momentary expression of extreme alarm, but she recovered herself almost immediately and gave him her hand as if she expected him to kiss it, which he did, though he was enraged with himself the next instant for doing so.

"*Quel plaisir*, to meet the famous Monsieur Carrington!" the Countess said condescendingly. "Of course one has heard of your travels to the most exotic quarters of the globe —"

"Yes, it's strange that our paths have never crossed before, *Countess*!" said Jasper, who had made up his mind to be the soul of discretion and not to utter a word that might upset her, but found himself at once driven to retaliation by her tone of languid superiority. He had come to the Assembly Rooms prepared to rescue her, quite as much in the nick of time as he had in the case of the collapsed bridge, from the situation of extreme peril in which the Baroness's tottyheadedness had placed her; and instead he not only found her in no need of rescue, but even enjoying herself and behaving towards him as if he were merely one more besotted male come to pay homage to her.

The Countess meanwhile said sweetly, without appearing in the least disturbed by the significant manner in which he had spoken, that she dared say they had often been in the same places only at different times, after which unhelpful remark the conversation was at once interrupted by the arrival of Geraint, who had come, he said, to hold the Baroness to her promise that she would present him to the Countess.

The Countess professed herself to be delighted to meet Lord Prest, and made room for him beside her on the sofa by the simple expedient of sending the young man seated on her right to fetch another glass of lemonade for her. Jasper, who found it highly ridiculous to be obliged to stand hovering respectfully, in company with a throng of her admirers, over a young lady towards whom he had grown accustomed to behaving as unceremoniously as if she had been the youth she had been impersonating at Arcourt's Hall, still had no intention of leaving her unguarded in company with Geraint, and looked at his cousin so forbiddingly that Geraint, who was used to deferring to him, got up rather nervously and asked him if he would like his place.

"Is Monsieur Carrington then infirm, that he cannot stand?" the Countess enquired, looking solicitously up at Jasper.

"No, he is not," Jasper said, feeling a strong impulse to box her ears. He went on grimly, "I believe this is to be a waltz, *Countess*; will you do me the honour of standing up with me?"

"Thank you so very much," she said graciously. "Some other time, perhaps, Monsieur Carrington. I should like now to dance rather with Lord Prest, as a reward for his being so very *gentil* as to offer to give up his place to you."

Geraint, delighted, proudly gave her his arm to lead her onto the floor, which irritated Jasper so much that he immediately went off and asked Peggy Falkirk to dance. She was looking lovelier than ever that evening in celestial blue crape with an aquamarine parure, and turned down several other applicants for the waltz in order to give her hand to Jasper.

"I see you have been talking to the Countess

Móra," she said, as they whirled off together to the intoxicating strains of the dance. "Shall you lose your heart to her, I wonder, as a great many of our other beaux seem to have done already?"

Jasper said there was no danger of that.

"Well, I don't know; she is very attractive," Peggy said. "Who in the world *is* she, by the bye? One hears the most extraordinary tales. But then, I daresay, unless the Baroness has taken you into her confidence, you know no more than the rest of us. She is being amazingly discreet, for once. Even Aunt Honoria could get nothing out of her."

Jasper looked down at her. It occurred to him suddenly that, in bringing young Miss Henry to England, he had laid a train that might well lead to a powder-keg, and that, as it appeared he was going to be able to exercise only the most imperfect control over either her or the Baroness, it behooved him to enlist a few allies. He had known Peggy Falkirk since the days when she had been Peggy Prest, a beautiful, blue-eyed child, always of an angelic temper and with a conscience elastic enough to allow her to support him loyally when he was trying to wriggle out of some scrape he had got himself into.

"Listen, Peggy," he said to her commandingly, "I want your help."

"*My* help?" Peggy raised her enormous blue eyes, now filled with mild surprise, to his face.

"Yes. I can't explain, but I've got myself into the devil of a coil. This is what I want you to do. If you hear of anything havey-cavey — anything at all, do you understand? — going on between your dear aunt Honoria and that fellow Croil that has to do with Giles Arcourt, will you let me know of it at once?''

"With *Giles*? But what could there possibly — ?''

"Never mind that. Just promise to tell me.''

"Of course I shall promise, Jasper, but I can't see how there could possibly be anything — ''

Jasper reflected that, for a girl who had spent most of her life under the same roof with a woman whose chief occupation had always been deception of one sort or another, she had managed to remain extraordinarily innocent, not to say stupid; but he was fond of Peggy, so he banished the thought. After all, she waltzed beautifully, and so, feeling that he deserved some reward for having behaved quite well through an evening that had held a series of very nasty shocks for him, he forgot about his troubles for the time being and gave himself up to the pleasures of the dance.

EIGHT

Meanwhile, Rolande, waltzing with Geriant, was able
to see clearly, as she and her partner whirled past Jasper
and *his* partner on the polished floor, just how well he
was enjoying himself. She had been congratulating
herself that she had come off very nicely in her meeting
with him a few minutes before, considering that she had
behaved with a good deal of aplomb and had managed
a clever escape from the trap he had laid for her in asking her to dance, for she knew that he would have done
nothing but ring a peal over her as long as the music had
lasted.

But now, perversely, she wished she had not
refused him; for some reason it was decidedly unpleasant to her to see his fair head bent so intimately
over Mrs. Falkirk's, and to note that the two of them
were engaged in what appeared to be a decidedly con-
fidential conversation.

"Is Mrs. Falkirk your cousin?" she asked Geraint

suddenly. "She is very beautiful, isn't she? Is she a widow?"

Geraint said yes, she was his cousin, yes, she was very beautiful, and yes, she was a widow.

"Is she Monsieur Carrington's cousin, also?" Rolande asked.

Geraint said no, he was on the other side of the family. He, Geraint, was in that first intoxicating stage of love in which every word the adored object utters is perceived to be fraught with some peculiar and exquisite meaning; and it appeared to him that the Countess's interest in his family tree was evidence of such a beautiful nature, so truly condescending, so little fixed upon self, that his admiration for her began to pass all reasonable bounds.

"But they are very good friends, then — *n'est-ce pas*?" Roande persevered, in a tone that might have seemed to him, in any other woman, a trifle cross. "Is he perhaps betrothed to her?"

"Betrothed to her? Jasper?" Geraint looked a little startled. "Oh, no. I shouldn't think Jasper would like being betrothed to anyone," he said.

"Indeed!" said Rolande. She was not sure whether the peculiar sensation this statement had caused in her was due to relief or to disappointment, both of which emotions appeared to be mixed up in it in a rather disagreeable way. "Why not?" she demanded, after a moment.

Geraint, who was growing a bit tired of talking about his cousin Jasper, and felt, besides, that the subject was beginning to tread on delicate ground in view of the fact that a complete answer to this last question must necessarily involve a discussion of Jasper's notoriously fickle nature where women were concerned, said vaguely that he dared say that sort of thing wasn't quite in his line.

"Indeed!" said Rolande again.

"Geraint thought she looked disapproving, and hastened to turn the subject.

During this time, Giles Arcourt, who had been jealously keeping watch on the Countess with a view to asking her to dance himself, was dodging about from one side of the room to the other, hoping to place himself in a strategic situation so that when the music stopped he would be in a proper position to make his request before anyone else did. He was not inspired in this endeavour by the same tender feelings that were animating Geraint, but, having been highly flattered by the Countess's having singled him out for her special attention, he was determined to take every advantage of the partiality she had displayed for him to enhance the position of prominence in which it had placed him.

Unfortunately, Rolande, who had discovered in her talk with him that he had the cunning of a thoroughly selfish mind in steering clear of conversational pitfalls likely to cause him trouble of any sort, had made up her mind not to waste any more of her time on him that evening, and was trying to manoeuvre herself into a position in which Jasper might renew his solicitation for her to stand up with him for the next dance.

But Jasper, casting not a glance in her direction at the end of the waltz, went off instead, after relinquishing Peggy Falkirk to another partner, to the sofa upon which Lady Prest had established herself, and was shortly to be seen seated beside her there, engaged in apparently amicable conversation with her. Rolande, disappointed, yielded to the entreaties of Lord Hoult and allowed herself to be led into a set of country dances by him, while Giles, also disappointed, went off into a corner to sulk.

"I see you have made the acquaintance of Louisa's mysterious Countess," Lady Prest said to Jasper as he seated himself beside her. "What do you make of her?"

"Nothing at all — nor she of me," said Jasper. "I asked her to dance, thinking I might delve into the mystery while we waltzed, but she would have none of me. It seems she prefers Geraint."

Lady Prest shrugged, looking at once pleased (it was not often that Geraint succeeded in cutting out his more dashing cousin) and disapproving.

"Foolish boy!" she said. "He is a romantic at heart, like his father." Jasper, who had only the vaguest of remembrances of the late Lord Prest, who had died when he, Jasper, was five years of age, felt that if Lady Prest's statement were true that gentleman must have had a very discouraging marriage. "There is something vaguely familiar to me about her face," Lady Prest went on in a dissatisfied tone, "but I can't think whom it reminds me of — someone I once met abroad, I daresay. It will come to me sooner or later, no doubt" — (Jasper devoutly hoped it would not) — "and that may give me a clew to her identity. *Not* Hanoverian in the least, I should think, in spite of that absurd rumour about the Regent."

"Oh, I don't know," said Jasper. "There's Cumberland; he's not at all like the rest of the stable. Besides, she may resemble the Hungarian side of the family."

Lady Prest primmed her lips slightly, as if to indicate that she felt that the Duke of Cumberland, definitely the black sheep among the Regent's large family of brothers and widely rumoured to have murdered his valet, was not a suitable subject for a conversation with a lady.

"But what I really wanted to ask you about, my dear Jasper," she went on at once, in her most staid and regal way, "is another very odd rumour that has come to my ears — that you have a young man staying at Arcourt's Hall who it is said may be attempting to impose upon you by claiming that *he* is actually Giles Arcourt. I daresay there can be no truth in such a very peculiar tale?"

Jasper said there was no truth in it whatever.

"Ah!" said Lady Prest, managing to convey a good deal of polite incredulity in the utterance of this single syllable. "Then there is no young man staying at the Hall?"

"Not any longer, there isn't," Jasper said. "He's gone back to Brussels — met with a couple of rather nasty accidents and decided the neighbourhood wasn't healthy for him. He's a Belgian, by the way — nothing in the world to do with Giles Arcourt."

"Oh?" said Lady Prest, demonstrating to Jasper that this monosyllable, too, could be effectively used to display disbelief. "Well, that is very odd, isn' it?"

"That he's gone to Brussels? I don't see that," Jasper said reasonably. "I daresay a good many Belgians go to Brussels at one time or another."

"Don't," said Lady Prest coldly, "be flippant, Jasper dear. You know precisely what I am speaking of. Does it not seem extremely odd to you that you should have had a young man staying with you who bears such a very marked resemblance to my brother John's late wife?"

Oh, so we're out in the open now, are we? Jasper thought. *Well, you'll get nothing from me, dear Aunt.*

Aloud, he said, "Does he? Queer, *I've* never noticed that. I must have a good look at him the next time I see him. Extraordinary coincidence that."

"Extraordinary," said Lady Prest dryly.

"If I *had* noticed it," Jasper pressed on, still appearing quite unperturbed, "I might have been tempted to take him to London and see what your legal bigwigs might make of him. Not that he hasn't a perfectly good pedigree of his own but, after all, eight million pounds is eight million pounds, and a fellow might be quite willing to take on a new identity to get his hands on such a sum, besides being deuced grateful to anyone who helped him do it. I rather imagine you're counting on that sort of thing — the gratitude, I mean — in the case of your own Giles Arcourt, aren't you?"

Lady Prest, looking utterly revolted at having such mercenary motives attributed to her, said stiffly that her only consideration in the entire affair was that of restoring her dear brother's son to his rightful inheritance, but was unable to prevent herself from adding rather acidly that she hoped Jasper would remember that resemblances counted for very little in the Law.

"There have been instances," she said, "of young persons of very low degree who have borne a most striking resemblance to men of the highest wealth and position, without having the least *legitimate* claim upon them — "

Jasper, who had an idea that the unusually close resemblance between Rolande and the late Mrs. John Arcourt might be due to a situation of this sort, as it was not beyond the bounds of possibility that one of the latter's ancestors might have taken a somewhat inordinate interest in the theatre, or at least in one of its ornaments in the shape of a Thespian ancestress of Rolande's mama's, said he dared say that was true, but he was surprised at her indelicacy in bringing it up.

"I always supposed that you were of the old school," he said, "and decried our modern habit of frank speaking on such subjects. But you are quite as bad as Cousin Louisa. Another of my illusions gone!"

He got up, ignoring the fulminating look she turned upon him, and, bowing to her, strolled away to seek the Baroness, with whom he felt the need of consultation. He did not flatter himself that his blanket denial to Lady Prest of any connexion between the Arcourt Will and the youth he had recently had staying with him at Arcourt's Hall had carried any conviction with her, and, though it seemed extremely unlikely to him that either she or Croil would be ingenious enough to find out the relationship between that youth and the Countess Móra, he felt that it behooved him and the Baroness to put their heads together at once and devise some safer disguise for Rolande.

101

Fortunately, he found the Baroness being besieged by old General Pusey, and exceedingly pleased to be rescued from him.

"I saw you talking to Honoria," she said, as soon as they were rid of the General. "What did she say to you? She hasn't suspected that the Countess Móra is really Giles Arcourt, has she?"

"Not at present," Jasper said. "But she does think she reminds her of someone she knows. Where can we go? I want to talk to you."

The Baroness looked round, said that when a set was forming, as it was at present, there was never anyone in the small anteroom opening from the ballroom behind her, and led the way through the doorway.

"Now before you begin pinching at me again for allowing Rolande to enter on this new masquerade," she said at once, "let me tell you, dearest Jasper, that it was all a matter of the merest chance. I had sent her off, you see, to let Disbrey try what she could do in turning her into a Hungarian, and when she — Rolande, of course, not Disbrey — came down to the drawing room to show me how she looked, there, by the unluckiest chance, were Honoria and Peggy sitting with me. Of course, I *had* to say something, so I simply invented the Countess Móra. And I must say the dear girl took me up splendidly. As a matter of fact, she didn't miss a cue."

"Well, she's an actress, isn't she?" said Jasper, ungraciously refusing to join in her encomium upon Rolande's cleverness. "But why a Hungarian, in heaven's name? What if she meets a real one? Does she know a word of the language?"

"Oh, I should think so," said the Baroness. "She seems to have lived all over Europe, and she has a very quick ear. Do you remember that Baranyi woman whose husband was attached to the Austrian Embassy a few years ago and carried on *à suivie* flirtations with every male in sight? But of course you do; you were one of them. Rolande sounds exactly like her, if you have noticed."

Jasper said rather grimly that he had noticed, and that he had also noticed that she was behaving exactly like her, as well.

"Yes, she has really astonished me," the Baroness said complacently. "I should never have believed that she could act the part so well. She was even casting out lures to Honoria's Giles Arcourt before you arrived — really very clever of her, for there is no telling what a pretty woman cannot get out of a young fool in the way of information if she sets her mind to it. *Not* that he seems the type to tumble head-over-ears in love with her, or with anyone else — a nasty, scrambling little creature, so puffed up with conceit over his own finery that he has no thought to spare for anything beyond it. I wonder that even Honoria has the face to attempt to thrust him on the family. Did she say anything to you about *your* Giles Arcourt, by the bye?"

"She did," said Jasper. "She knows all about the young man I had staying at the Hall who bears such a very unusual resemblance to the late Mrs. John Arcourt — as you will no doubt not be surprised to learn. Of course it would have done no good for me to deny it, so I said he had gone back to Brussels."

"But how clever of you, darling Jasper!"

"Not so very clever. She obviously didn't believe me. It's Lombard Street to a China orange she has Croil looking for him already — which brings me to our present problem. What the devil are we to do now with that curst chit? She can't go on playing this bogus Countess directly under Aunt Honoria's nose."

"But, my dear Jasper, why can't she? If you wish my opinion, it is precisely the safest place for her — directly under Honoria's nose, that is. Even Honoria would not have the audacity to attempt such a thing, so she will certainly not suspect us of it. Besides, it will give us the very best opportunity to keep her — that is, Rolande — constantly under observation, which we should not have if we sent her anywhere else. She will continue to stay with me, of course, and as for you — you have only to pretend you have conceived a *grande passion* for her to give you a perfect excuse to follow her about whenever she appears in public —"

"A *what*?" interrupted Jasper, looking revolted.

"Yes, I know you have never conceived one for any female before this," the Baroness said placidly, "but really, dear boy, a simple flirtation will not cover the situation if you are to pursue her as relentlessly as poor Caro Lamb pursued Byron. No one thought it in the least unusual, you know, to see her dressed as a page-boy, waiting for him for hours, with all the grooms and coachmen, outside a house where he was attending a ball —"

"Well, I am not going to wait for hours for Miss Henry *in*side or *out*side of any house in Brighton!" said Jasper, looking extremely exasperated. "Nor shall I pretend to a *grande passion* for her —"

104

"A *grande passion* for whom?" Rolande's voice enquired behind them.

The conspirators started. She had come in without their having heard her, and, like all people who have been caught acting imprudently, they both at once accused *her* of imprudence.

"You should not have come in here!" the Baroness scolded her, and Jasper said coldly, "I should imagine you are disappointing at least one of the many admirers you appear to have collected this evening by coming here, *Countess*."

"If you call me *Countess* once more in that perfectly odious tone, I shall hit you," Rolande announced, frowning at Jasper. "Are you going to pretend to have a *grande passion* for me? Because I can tell you, if you are, that I should not like that in the least."

"You may put your mind to rest," said Jasper austerely. "Nothing would induce me to make such a cake of myself."

"I do not know why you say 'making a cake,' " said Rolande, looking offended. "Your cousin, Lord Prest — he is very *gentil*, very *comme il faut*, and *he* does not consider it *making a cake* to pay marked attentions to me."

In moments of stress Rolande's English always became more French.

Jasper, however, merely smiled and shrugged in a disparaging manner.

"Oh — Geraint!" he said. "He is always falling top-over-tail in love with one girl or another. The trouble is that he never does anything about it."

"He will do something about *me*, if I wish him

to!'' Rolande said darkly. "If I wish him to, he will marry me, and then *I* shall be very rich because *he* will have the eight million pounds and you will have nothing!''

"Why, you little vixen — !'' Jasper began, but the Baroness at once stepped into the breach with pacifying words.

"Now, now — we must not quarrel,'' she said. "*So* tiresome, not to say stupid, for it is exactly what Honoria would wish us to do. Of course you cannot marry Geraint, my dear Rolande; he never moves without his mother's consent, and I can assure you that she has far higher game in mind for him than a little French actress, even though your grandfather *was* a baronet. As for you, dearest Jasper,'' she went on, turning to him, "I consider that pretending to have a *grande passion* for Rolande is such a small price to pay for eight million pounds that it has me in the greatest puzzle to understand why you should boggle at it.''

"But I don't wish him to — '' Rolande began rebelliously.

"Not wish him to! But of course you do!'' the Baroness said reprovingly. "You must remember, dear child, that it always adds to a female's consequence to have any man, no matter how personally repugnant to her, desperately in love with her. And you need not give Jasper the slightest encouragement, you know; indeed, the more disdain you show towards him, the more reason he will have to follow you about and hungrily watch your every movement — ''

But here she was interrupted by Jasper, who said

that he considered it disgusting for a man to look hungrily at any woman, more or less as if he were a dog and she a bone, but that if he must do it, he must, especially as it seemed the only possible way to keep the Countess Móra under surveillance. He then added that he had no intention of allowing her to continue in her present masquerade any longer than it would take him to find a more secure place of safety for her and walked off into the ballroom.

"I do think men are the most tiresome creatures!" said the Baroness to Rolande when he had gone. "They have absolutely no sense of romance, or adventure — always so prosaic and common-sensical, besides getting in a black rage with one when one is only trying to be helpful. Jasper hasn't the least appreciation, it seems to me, of how very clever we both have been, and of what an enormously advantageous situation we have placed him in. Here you have Honoria's Giles Arcourt positively dangling at your shoe-strings, so that heaven knows what may be got out of him — and Jasper talks of finding a more secure place of safety for you! It would serve him exactly right if we sat still and did nothing at all — but I *do* think that would be so very dull; don't you, my dear?"

Rolande said she did, and that she had no intention of going anywhere at all until she had done her possible to unmask the bogus Giles.

"He seems to me to be stupid but very sly," she said. "We shall have to make a plan, I think, because I do not believe it is possible he will fall in love with me *à corps perdu* and therefore be very indiscreet in telling me his secrets — not even though I am wearing such a beautiful gown as this and have been made to look so alluring by Disbrey.''

She glanced complacently but with an air of entire detachment at her reflection in the pier glass before which she stood, and the Baroness saw with some amusement that she evidently considered the Countess Móra a creature quite apart from the real Rolande Henry. Decidedly, she thought, the girl was an original, one of those extraordinarily interesting people who could always be counted upon to see things from an unexpected point of view, and it would be a great loss to the social scene if she were to disappear from it forever, once she had succeeded (as the Baroness was quite sure she would) in accomplishing the purpose for which Jasper had brought her to England.

A suitable marriage, she thought, would solve the problem — to someone to whom her rather ambiguous background would not matter a jot; but outside of Jasper she could think of no one, on the spur of the moment, who possessed this sort of character, and it was out of the question, of course, to expect Jasper to marry anyone. She thought, on the whole, that it might be best to encourage young Lord Hoult. He was of age, and therefore in a position to snap his fingers at family opposition, and men had been know to marry very oddly when under the influence of a genuine inclination. Look, for example, she said to herself, at Charles James Fox and Mrs. Armistead.

NINE

On the following morning the Baroness and Rolande, full of plans for entering into the social life of Brighton for the purposes each had in mind — the entrapment of Giles Arcourt in the case of both ladies, with the additional motive of finding a suitable husband for Rolande in the case of the Baroness — were up and abroad at the earliest fashionable hour. The Baroness had the slightly eccentric but delightful habit of driving herself everywhere in Brighton in a small carriage drawn by ponies no larger than Kamtschatkadale dogs, and it was in this conveyance that they presently arrived at Donaldson's Library. First, however, they had driven along the sea-front to enjoy a view of sparkling blue waters under a bright July sun and to display their own dashing toilettes of, respectively, purple-blue jaconet muslin and pink-and-cherry-striped Chinese crape to the admiring gaze of all the promenaders strolling there — the dandies in blue coats with enormously high collars, the smart young officers, and the ladies of various shapes and sizes, from sylphs to buxom Junos, but all attired alike in clinging, high-waisted gowns and large hats.

Donaldson's Library, which stood on the Steyne in the centre of Brighton's most fashionable district, was a popular meeting-place for those members of the *ton* who were interested in obtaining the latest novel the newest issue of a London periodical, or the most recent *on-dit* concerning fellow-members of their set; and in one of its elegant and spacious rooms the Baroness, not to her surprise, found the party she was seeking. It consisted of Peggy Falkirk, the bogus Giles Arcourt, and Lady Prest. A thin, dry, middle-aged man, who looked like an immensely superior butler with a very low opinion of his employer, rounded out the group. Geraint was lounging in a chair across the room, talking to a young lady in blue, but upon seeing the Countess Móra made his excuses with more rapidity than civility and came at once to join them.

"This," the Baroness had remarked *sotto voce* to Rolande as they had approached the little group, "is the acid test, my dear. The man, I must tell you, is *Croil.*"

The prospect of being obliged to carry out her impersonation of the Countess Móra in the presence of the man who had been held up to her as the chief architect of the plot against Jasper was a daunting one, but Rolande rose to the occasion. She gave him her most bored and condescending nod and then turned at once to Giles Arcourt and began to converse with him with the playful partiality of a woman of the world for a much younger favourite.

"But you have not come to call upon me this morning, as you promised!'' she accused him, in the slow, rich, caressing accent that the Baroness felt even Croil's sharp ears would not be able to identify as anything but the genuine Hungarian. ''What an ungrateful little *monstre* you are, to be sure! And now you will be expecting to sit beside me, is it not so? — at the concert which the dear Baroness says we shall attend this afternoon at Promenade Grove. But no, and no, I tell you! It shall not be! It is Lord Prest who shall sit beside me, and hold my fan, and perhaps bring me a glass of lemonade if the heat becomes oppressive —''

She turned a charming smile upon Geraint, who had been waiting with eager diffidence to pay his devoirs to her, and he at once stammered that he would be delighted, there was nothing he would like more than to escort her and his cousin Louisa to the concert. He was interrupted, however, by Giles Arcourt, who said indignantly that Geraint would do nothing of the sort, as he, Giles, had had every intention of calling upon the Countess at the earliest hour at which he had believed she would care to admit company after the fatigues of the previous evening, and of offering her his escort to any place of entertainment that she cared to visit during the course of the day.

Having embroiled the two young men in this dispute and seeing that Lady Prest was looking daggers at her, Rolande smiled benignly upon them all and drifted off to a table nearby to turn over the pages of the most recent issue of *La Belle Assemblée*.

Of course both her swains followed her at once, leaving the Baroness with Lady Prest, Mrs. Falkirk, and Croil.

"A most attractive young lady," said Croil in his precise, resonant, and well-modulated voice. It was generally felt in the profession that he might have been even more successful as a barrister than he was as a solicitor, since no judge or jury could be expected to be able to stand out against the combination of that noble voice and that butlerlike expression of Olympian contempt, which would infallibly make them all feel like sweeps. "If I may be permitted to say so," he continued in measured tones, "she bears a remarkable resemblance to the late Mrs. John Arcourt."

The Baroness felt her heart give a decided thump and tried her best to look as if this statement did not interest her in the least. At the same time she saw her cousin Honoria sit up even straighter than she had been doing, if that was possible, and look quickly across the room at Rolande.

"But you are quite right, Mr. Croil!" she exclaimed. "Of course! I thought the moment I met her that she reminded me of someone I knew, and you have put your finger upon it exactly!"

Croil bowed slightly, accepting with aplomb this tribute to his perspicacity. The Baroness, realising that the whole plot she and Rolande were about to hatch would be ruined if she did not succeed in casting doubt upon this suspicious resemblance at once, said critically that she could not perceive it.

"Perhaps it is because I see her so very clearly as her mother's daughter," she said, in as sentimental a tone as she could call up on the spur of the moment. "Dear Höja had the same camellia-pallor and intriguing, slightly slanted eyes — there is Tartar blood there, you see — and the same masses of jet-black hair. I confess there is nothing in all this that seems to me to bear the least resemblance to poor John's wife.''

Lady Prest, looking dissatisfied, said she could not argue with that, but it seemed to her, all the same, that there really *was* a resemblance.

"Gammon!" said the Baroness, with the bracing frankness she had used towards her cousin when they had both been in short frocks with their hair tied up with ribbons. "You have windmills in your head, Honoria. I hear you have been plaguing Jasper about some foreign young man he had staying with him at the Hall, saying *he* resembled Marie-Jeanne, too. It appears to be some sort of obsession with you at present.''

Lady Prest, looking rather sulky — the Baroness was the only person who could make her feel she was a very unimportant and not very clever woman — said that Mr. Croil had noticed the resemblance first.

"If *I* were Mr. Croil," said the Baroness, fixing him with the severe gaze that had quelled the pretensions of dozens of impeccable butlers and majordomos all over the globe, "*I* should probably see Mrs. John Arcourt in every face I looked into, too, like Macbeth and Banquo. *Not* that I suspect Mr. Croil of murdering Marie-Jeanne, of course, but after all he *was* the *one* who brought that perfectly horrid boy over from Vienna and told you he was her son — Ah, good morning, Colonel McMahon!" she broke off to address an ugly little man in a blue and buff uniform, who had just come into the room. "Is the Regent expected soon in

Brighton? One would not hope to find *you* here if that were not the case.''

She moved off with the Regent's secretary, whom she detested, to another part of the room, hoping that she had sufficiently confused the issue of whether the Countess Móra really did resemble the late Mrs. John Arcourt, but not at all certain that she had done so. She could see Lady Prest and Croil with their heads together, and wondered unhappily if they were putting two and two together and coming to the unlikely conclusion that the elegant Countess might be the mysterious youth from Arcourt's Hall in disguise. Moreover, she had to ask herself, what was it that had brought Croil down from London to Brighton in the first place? Had he come to report in person to Lady Prest upon the disappearance of the mysterious youth from Arcourt's Hall, and his inability to discover his present whereabouts, or had he actually succeeded in tracing the missing youth to Brighton?

It was all very vexing and highly upsetting, and she wished Jasper were present so that she could take counsel with him. But a message sent to the Old Ship that morning had elicited only the unsatisfactory information that Mr. Carrington had been seen driving off from the inn in his curricle at an early hour, and that no sort of message had been left for her. The one crumb of comfort provided her was the certainty that, wherever he had gone, he had not left Brighton for good, for he had not given up his room at the Old Ship.

Still, it was very thoughtless of him, she could not help feeling, to abandon her and Rolande to the

machinations of Croil and Lady Prest, and she determined to take him severely to task for his dereliction of
duty when next she saw him.

She judged it prudent, meanwhile, to remove
Rolande immediately from the dangerous vicinity of
Croil, and as soon as she was able to detach her from
her two determined admirers — who had been joined,
she saw with some satisfaction, by Lord Hoult — she
drove her away from the Library in her little pony-
carriage.

When they had reached home, she at once
described to Rolande the conversation she had had with
Croil and Lady Prest.

"I do think," she said, "that if we are to try to get
any information from Honoria's Giles Arcourt we had
best move quickly, for it is perfectly obvious that she is
already growing suspicious of you. And, while I can be
fairly certain of being able to diddle Honoria, Croil is
another matter. He looks the picture of respectability,
but he is actually a very sinister creature, I have heard,
with a diabolically clever mind and really uncanny
powers of perception. You can't think what a turn it
gave me at the Library when he said, almost the first
moment he clapped eyes upon you, that you resembled
Mrs. John Arcourt."

Rolande said she had been thinking about what
they should do, too, and it had come to her like an in-
spiration that their best hope lay, not in cajoling the
false Giles Arcourt, but in frightening him.

"He has been taught very well what he is to say
about his past life, it seems to me," she said, "and

never makes the least mistake when one questions him. But he is not very courageous, I think, and if he were to receive a severe shock, it might alter matters."

"A shock?" The Baroness looked intrigued. "But of what sort — ?"

"I have thought of that, too," said Rolande proudly. "*Ecoutez.*"

And she proceeded to lay before the Baroness a plan of such daring and ingenuity that even that lady, who was famed for those qualities herself, was seized with admiration.

"But, my dear, we can't possibly!" she recovered her common sense sufficiently to protest when her first enthusiasm had subsided somewhat. "Only think what Jasper will say if we take such a risk! He will murder us both!"

"Ah, bah! I am not afraid of Mr. Carrington," Rolande said loftily. "Besides, he will know nothing about it until it is all over and we have succeeded in frightening that horrid boy into admitting that he is not Giles Arcourt. And then Mr. Carrington will not be able to be angry, because he will be so very grateful to us."

The Baroness said doubtfully that it was obvious she, Rolande, did not know Jasper very well, because in her experience he was quite capable of being extremely disagreeable when one did something he didn't wish one to do, no matter how well-intentioned one was. Like the time she and Lebanoff had tried to surprise him, she said, by inviting to dinner the Italian countess he had been so fond of in Rome when she had turned up in St. Petersburg, and placing her beside him, only to discover that they were by that time at daggers' ends with each other.

"As if I could have known the woman would make that dreadful scene!" she defended herself. "But Jasper was so rude to me over it that Lebanoff wanted to call him out, which would have been quite absurd, of course, since it was all in the family. And I will say that he — that is, Jasper — brought me a delicious little piece of *mille-fleurs* porcelain the next day as a peace offering. But all the same, I do *not* advise you to carry out this plan of yours without first consulting him, my dear."

Rolande said obstinately that that was all very well, but, as the Baroness herself had admitted, it was of the highest importance for them to act quickly, and meanwhile, where was Jasper for her to consult? — even if she wished to consult him, which she did not.

"All he is thinking of," she said, "is sending me away, which will ruin everything. And I don't *wish* to be sent away."

The Baroness, who was growing very fond of Rolande, said she didn't wish her to be sent away, either, and little by little allowed herself to be persuaded, somewhat against her better judgement, to enter as a fellow-conspirator into the plan that Rolande had proposed.

After all, she consoled herself, there was scarcely any risk involved if the plan succeeded, as they would then be rid once and for all of Honoria's Giles Arcourt, so that Honoria, with her hope of obtaining the Arcourt fortune through him at an end, would have no further incentive to harm Jasper's Giles Arcourt. And if it did *not* succeed, it would mean only that it would be even more expedient for the Countess Móra to disappear quickly, which, as this was what Jasper himself desired, would leave him nothing to object to.

TEN

Accordingly, when Rolande and the Baroness set out for Promenade Grove that afternoon, gallanted by both Geraint and Giles, who were scarcely on speaking terms by this time owing to their dispute over who was to be permitted to sit beside the Countess (they had finally compromised on sitting one on each side), their plan was fully matured. Jasper had not appeared, nor had any word been received from him, so that it seemed unlikely that interference could be expected from that quarter, which the Baroness could not help feeling served him right for deserting them in their hour of need.

"A *grande passion*, indeed!" she snorted to Rolande. "No one can have conceived the least notion that he cares tuppence for you! I shall certainly have a word with that young man when he turns up — *if* he ever does!"

As it was a delicious summer afternoon, warm and still, with the softest of breezes rippling the gentle surf along the sea-front, the ladies chose to walk to the Grove, which was only a short distance from the house on the Steyne, lying on the southwestern side of the onion-shaped domes and minarets of the Regent's Marine Pavilion. This fantastic edifice was, as usual, undergoing a process of alteration and renovation, the Regent having given *carte blanche* to John Nash, his architect, and to his decorators, Robert Jones and the Craces, father and son, with the result that two great new apartments, the Music Room and the Banqueting Room, both with elaborately painted domed ceilings, chandeliers like waterlilies, and enormous Chinese wall-paintings, were now the talk of Brighton. The Baroness, who was *au courant* of all the Royal gossip, said the Regent had already spent almost six hundred thousand pounds on improvements to the Pavilion, with the end not yet in sight, and that even the kitchens were ornamented with cast-iron columns in the form of palm trees.

At these words Giles looked much impressed, but Geraint, who had visited the Pavilion more than once in previous years, for the Regent was very fond of entertaining at small dinners, concerts, and receptions, said with a smile it was no wonder Prinny had decided upon a form of architecture and decoration reminiscent of the Indian and the Moorish, as it was his habit to keep the Pavilion so unbearably overheated that one always felt there as if one were in a semitropical country, at any rate.

He then apparently recollected the rumour that had gone round about the Countess's possible relationship to the Regent, coloured up scarlet, and began very quickly to point out to Rolande the beauties of Promenade Grove.

It was indeed a lovely spot, elaborately laid out with formal beds of luxuriantly growing flowers interspersed by leafy alleys and secluded bowers, with a wooden bandstand at its centre where an orchestra was just beginning to play gay waltzes and marches. Geraint and Giles busied themselves in finding seats for their ladies, and in a very short time Rolande found herself ensconced between the two of them, with the Baroness, rather out of it, seated on Geraint's right.

Not for nothing, however, had the two ladies laid their elaborate plans before they had left the house on the Steyne. For a short time they allowed matters to take their normal course, paying the same desultory sort of attention to the music as their neighbours were doing, while the two young men each made every effort to monopolise Rolande.

But presently Geraint, against all his inclinations, found himself attached, surrounded, and led away captive by the Baroness; or at least that was how it appeared to him. She dropped her fan; she misplaced her reticule; she demanded his advice on the purchase of a new pair of carriage horses; and every time he attempted to turn back to Rolande a new and more maddening intervention occurred, forcing him in common civility to return to the Baroness.

Meanwhile, Rolande and Giles Arcourt were conferring rapidly, in intimate undertones, and Geraint suddenly discovered, in the midst of his desperate and hurried efforts to extricate the Baroness's filmy scarf from the strings of her reticule, in which she had very cleverly managed to entangle it, that the two had risen and were walking off together.

Of course it was impossible for Geraint to fling down the pestilential scarf, run after them, and demand to be included in their stroll, so he ground his teeth as inaudibly as he could and went on disentangling the scarf, while Rolande and Giles disappeared round a turn in one of the zigzag paths.

What Rolande had said to bring about this state of events was, "I have something of the most serious to discuss with you, *mon petit*. Shall we walk a little away from the others? It requires privacy and the greatest of discretion, you see."

Giles, needing no second invitation for a tête-à-tête with the Countess, although obviously a trifle disturbed by the portentiousness of her tone, immediately rose, and in a few moments they were strolling together along the now deserted paths leading away from the centre of the Grove. The music came more faintly to their ears; they were quite alone; and Rolande, leading the way to a rustic bench in one of the many small bowers the Grove contained, sat down upon it and motioned to her companion to place himself beside her.

He promptly did so, and then, seizing her hand, began with precocious ardour to cover it with kisses. Rolande, who would have liked very much to snatch it away from him and put it to better use in boxing his ears, restrained herself and put on a mournful air.

"Alas, *mon petit*, are you so fond of me, then?" she asked. "And I of you, I confess — which is why I feel I must warn you of the great danger that hangs over

122

you. It would tear my heart to see *mon petit monstre* led off in disgrace to gaol, or perhaps even — who knows what may happen in this heathen country? — to the gallows.''

"To the gallows?" Giles Arcourt abruptly lost all interest in the hand he had a moment before been devouring with kisses and raised startled eyes to Rolande's face. "What are you saying? *Was sagen Sie?*" he asked rapidly, in German.

Rolande was pleased to see that his rather florid face had suddenly been drained of colour. She looked down pensively at the handle of the frivolous little Chinese sunshade she was carrying.

"But yes," she said. "The gallows, *mon cher*. Is it too much to expect that these barbarous people would proceed even to those lengths against someone who tried to defraud one of them of the sum of eight million pounds?"

Giles made a sort of gobbling, protesting noise, and Rolande looked up with interest to see that his face had again become as red as it had been white the moment before. The gobbling sounds resolved themselves into words, and she was able to distinguish a statement, uttered with great bravado but without much conviction, to the effect that he had not the least notion what she was talking about.

"Really?" said Rolande. "I had thought you were more clever, *mon petit*. Or have they not told you — Lady Prest and the so efficient Croil — that it is that amount that is involved in this little comedy you enact for them? What have they offered you for this impersonation, by the bye? A paltry sum, I wager, con-

123

sidering that it is *you*, not they, who will be caught in the toils of the Law when it is discovered that you are not really Giles Arcourt."

The youth sitting beside her took a deep breath, assumed an air of hauteur, and said of course he was Giles Arcourt.

"You have been listening," he said accusingly, "to Herr Carrington — *nicht wahr*? My aunt, Lady Prest, has warned me of him. He is a man of the most dangerous, she says, who will stop at nothing to defraud me of my inheritance."

"As to his being dangerous," Rolande said judicially, "I can believe that well. The Baroness, my good hostess, has already informed me of that, which is one good reason, *mon petit*, why I fear you are in such peril. *Naturellement*, if you tell me you are truly Giles Arcourt, I must believe you — but I think you cannot be aware, my poor child, that Mr. Carrington has discovered another young man who claims that *he* is that person, and who bears, moreover, a truly uncanny resemblance to the lady who was your mother, or his mother — it confuses me to know how to put it. You have seen a portrait of the late Mrs. John Arcourt, perhaps?"

Giles, looking shaken, said that Lady Prest had several miniatures of her in her possession.

"*Eh bien*," said Rolande, "this youth of Mr. Carrington's has the same brilliantly blue eyes, the same odd dark-coppery hair, and the same features as the late Mrs. Arcourt. He was reared in Vienna, he says, by a family named Schmidt, who received the care of him when the couple who had brought him out of France died. They became so fond of him that they wished to keep him for their own son, and told him nothing of his true origin, so that it was only upon stumbling on some hidden documents a few months ago that he became aware that he was Giles Arcourt and not Johann Schmidt. At least, that is the story he tells — "

She had been observing her companion closely while she spoke, and was pleased to see that she had succeeded in shaking his composure to the extent that he had taken to biting his nails furiously, with an expression upon his face which showed he had almost forgotten her presence in his absorption in the problem her words had placed before him. But Croil, she thought, had chosen his tool carefully, for in a few moments the boy's face cleared and, shrugging his shoulders, he said with an air of forced indifference, "*Nun, wirklich*, you have been deceived, Countess! There is no such young man as you have described to me. This is an invention of Herr Carrington's, to frighten me into giving up my claim."

Rolande shook her head. "Oh no, *mon cher*," she said positively. "He is not an invention. In point of fact, he will be here in Brighton, I am assured, today. The Baroness is receiving him into her house this evening — as a favour to Mr. Carrington, you understand, and in the strictest secrecy, for the time being. And after that — who knows, *mon pauvre enfant*, what will become of you when he has revealed himself at the proper time and these English vultures of the Law have you in their talons? It will be a simple matter then for

Lady Prest and the man Croil to claim that you have deceived them as you have deceived everyone else, and to leave you to bear the brunt of prosecution alone."

Giles Arcourt's face resumed its hunted look.

"You are positive of this? — that this young man exists?"

"Quite positive. If you would like to see him for yourself, you have only to call at the Baroness's house this evening — well after dark, *bien entendu* — to meet him. Mr. Carrington, of course, would be very angry if he knew I had disclosed this matter to you, but he will not be there this evening and the Baroness is almost as well disposed towards you as I am; she too does not wish you to be placed in a position where you will be obliged to pay for the wicked deception Lady Prest and Croil have practised upon you. Poor boy — you are very young; you do not know the world! These people have used you for their own purposes, taking advantage of your innocence — and they will leave you, in the end, to pay the price of their perfidy, while they themselves go free!"

Not for nothing, Rolande thought with satisfaction, had she frequently heard her mother declaiming the lines of the wronged heroines in the melodramatic pieces in which she had attained her greatest successes in the theatre; she doubted that even *Maman* could have uttered those final phrases with more feeling. And obviously they had made a deep impression upon Giles, who was back at chewing his finger-ends once more.

But, as a pupil of Croil, he was more difficult to shake than she had hoped, and she saw in a few moments that she would no doubt be obliged to go through with the whole of the plan she and the Baroness had concocted, and reveal *their* Giles Arcourt to him at the house that evening, before he would break down completely and confess his duplicity.

At any rate, however, it was obvious that Rolande had brought him to the point of serious doubt as to the wisdom of continuing his masquerade, for he said to her presently, with an air of having arrived at a difficult decision, "Very well! I shall come, then, to the house of the Baroness this evening and see this young man for myself."

"Good!" said Rolande. "But do not, I earnestly beg you, *mon petit*, bring with you Croil, or Lady Prest. If one of them were to appear with you, I can assure you that you would be met with nothing but denials of this young man's existence. *They* already know, I must tell you, that there is such a young man — though they have been very careful, I daresay, to keep that information from *you* — and the truth is that they would like nothing better than to get him out of the way, by fair means or foul. This is the reason, of course, why he does not yet wish to reveal himself publicly. You understand all this perfectly?"

Giles Arcourt looked as if he did not understand it even imperfectly, but Rolande, feeling that it was best to break off the discussion at this point, put an end to it by rising and leading him back to the Baroness and Geraint, who they found had now been joined by Jasper.

"What do you think?" the Baroness said as they

came up. "Jasper has been to Shoreham today and bought a yacht. He says we shall all go for an excursion on it very soon."

"A yacht?" said Rolande. She regarded Jasper suspiciously; he was looking very smug, she thought. "How could you buy a yacht?" she demanded. "They are expensive, and you have no money."

"Well, it isn't a very good yacht," Jasper said vaguely. "It belonged to Johnnie Harte; he's all to pieces, you know, and was obliged to raise the recruits, so I said I'd buy it. Won't you sit down here beside me, *Countess*? I've been pining to see you all day; nothing but this yacht affair could have torn me away from your side."

The Baroness looked at him scornfully; if this, her beady black eyes eloquently said, was a modern young man's idea of expressing a *grande passion*, she thanked God she belonged to an older generation.

Rolande, too, appeared less than satisfied with Jasper's ardour, and said as there was not room now for both her and Giles in the group, she and he would sit elsewhere.

"Nonsense!" said Jasper. "There is plenty of room. I shall sit on the ground at your feet in the very agreeable fashion I see has been adopted lately in the most fashionable drawing rooms by many of our young sprigs. One or two, I have observed, have even been daring enough to recline with their heads in their ladies' laps — but I daresay that would be considered rather too much by you?"

Rolande said with some emphasis that it would, but could not forbear taking the seat he had given up for her. He promptly sat down at her feet and enquired whether she intended to visit the theatre that evening, as there was no ball at the Assembly Rooms of either the Castle Inn or the Old Ship.

"I do not think so," Rolande said, mindful of her engagement for that evening with Giles Arcourt.

"The card-assembly, then?"

The Baroness, who had gathered from the expressive glance cast at her by Rolande as she had returned from her tête-à-tête with Giles, that their plan was well in train, intervened at this point to say with authority that she and Rolande would go nowhere that evening, being quite fatigued and feeling it necessary to recruit their forces for the breakfast being given the following day by Lord Hoult and a young friend of his, Sir Robert Carlisle.

"For what?" said Jasper incredulously, for a "breakfast," in spite of its name, did not begin until three or four in the afternoon, and even though it might go on until well past midnight he could see no valid reason why his cousin Louisa, who could put in an appearance at half a dozen balls in one evening without feeling fatigue, or the young and healthy Miss Henry, should find it necessary to remain at home all evening in order to be able to cope with it.

The Baroness, however, said firmly that such was the case, and, furthermore, that they did not care to see company that evening, which made Jasper even more certain that she and Rolande were concocting something they did not wish him to know about. But he was prudent enough to keep such thoughts to himself, and to continue instead his very offhand and one-sided flirtation with Rolande, which enraged Geraint to a point of silent fury, as he considered his cousin's manner insufficiently respectful of the lovely and possibly royal Countess Móra.

The Countess herself, however, as well as the Baroness, remained very well satisfied with the progress of their plot when, back at the house on the Steyne, the former had confided the results of her tête-à-tête with Giles Arcourt, and they made their preparations for the evening in the most sanguine hope that, at its conclusion, they would have removed Lady Prest's pretender to the Arcourt fortune once and for all from the scene.

ELEVEN

As if even the weather were in league to further their plans, it came on to storm that evening. The wind rose to a rather alarming extent; huge dark cloud masses lowered over the sea; and at last a perfect torrent of rain poured down upon Brighton. It was scarcely probable, Rolande and the Baroness thought with satisfaction, that they would be disturbed by any visitors that evening, other than the one they were expecting. By the time darkness fell Rolande, attired once again as Giles Arcourt in breeches, coat, and boots, her short, dark-coppery hair brushed *au coup de vent* and her face scrubbed clean of the Countess Móra's elaborate *maquillage*, was waiting in her bedchamber for her cue to appear onstage, while the Baroness, seated below in a purposely dimly lit drawing room, attended the arrival of the second Giles Arcourt.

They had not long to wait. On the heels of a tremendous clap of thunder, Hendon, the Baroness's butler, trod into the drawing room to announce Mr.

Giles Arcourt, and a few moments later Giles himself entered, looking — the Baroness observed with satisfaction — more than a little apprehensive.

"Good evening, my dear boy!" she greeted him cordially. "How very good of you to come to us in all this rain! The Countess will be desolated to miss seeing you."

"To — to miss seeing me?" Another ferocious clap of thunder, which made the very candlesticks rattle, caused him to start nervously and interrupted the thread of his speech for a moment. "But I thought —" he began again, "I thought she —"

"Yes, I know all about it, dear boy; she has told me of your little talk this afternoon," the Baroness said soothingly. "Unfortunately, ever since she returned home from the Grove she has been afflicted with the most dreadful migraine — the sun, I fear: she is very susceptible to it — and I have persuaded her to retire early. Rest, I have found — rest, and a few drops of hartshorn — is the sovereign remedy in these cases. But of course," she added, seeing that Giles was looking very much taken aback by the Countess's unexpected defection, and even seemed upon the point of turning tail and leaving the house, "of course, you shall see the young man you came to meet, dear boy. He arrived here only a few hours ago, and I have been obliged to use a good deal of persuasion to induce him to see you. But, as the dear Countess explained to me that you could not bring yourself to believe you had been so grossly deceived by Lady Prest and Mr. Croil unless you saw the real Giles Arcourt with your own eyes, I felt there was no other way, and I finally brought him to realise that as well. He will be down in a few moments, I expect; I told Hendon to inform him as soon as you arrived. Wouldn't you care to sit down? You look so very tentative, standing there just inside the door.''

Giles, thus adjured, sat down on the edge of the chair nearest the door and looked rather miserably at a large portrait by Reynolds of the late Baron Lebanoff. The Baron, who was in full Court dress, appeared to be eyeing him sternly, much in the style, it seemed to him, of a judge upon the Bench.

"You didn't tell Lady Prest, of course?" the Baroness's voice broke in on his uneasy reverie.

He blinked at her. "*Bitte*?" he said. "Tell her what?"

"That you were going to see the real Giles Arcourt?"

A mulish look came into his face. "But *I* am the real Giles Arcourt," he said.

The Baroness, feeling it best not to argue with him, said, "Very well, then. To see the *other* Giles Arcourt."

"I did not tell her anything," Giles said. "I said merely that I was going to call on the Countess Móra." He added gloomily, "She did not like it."

"No, I daresay she didn't," agreed the Baroness. "She never does like anyone to do anything she has not told them to do. I am desperately sorry for Geraint and Peggy for that reason — they are both quite under her thumb, you know — and I should be sorry for you, too, if I thought it at all likely that you would be long remaining with her. She would be appointed your guardian, of course, if it were proved that you were actually her nephew, and you can't think, really, how disagreeable that would be — "

She broke off abruptly as a thunderclap so shattering that it seemed the very house was about to fall down about their ears sounded directly over their heads. At that very instant, as if he had materialised from the nether regions like the devil in the tale of Dr. Faustus, the door was flung open and upon the threshold there appeared, to the horrified eyes of Giles Arcourt, a youth in a coat of dandy russet, highly polished boots, and fawn-coloured breeches, a youth with odd, dark-coppery hair, whole features bore an uncanny resemblance to those he had seen in the miniatures of the late Mrs. John Arcourt that had been shown him by Lady Prest. For a moment the youth stood there scowling at him; then he strode into the room and, addressing the Baroness, said in curt, guttural accents, "You wished to see me, Cousin Louisa?"

"Yes," said the Baroness composedly, observing with satisfaction how the other Giles Arcourt nervously shrank back in his chair as the newcomer passed him. "This is — dear me, it is very difficult to know quite how to introduce you to each other, since you are both Giles Arcourt, or at least you both call yourselves so! But, at any rate, Giles dear, this is the young man whom your aunt Honoria and that dreadful man Croil have persuaded — *quite* unscrupulously and most unfairly — to say that *he* is Giles Arcourt, and I am sure he is very sorry for it now, and wishes he had not done it."

The latter part of this statement was vividly borne out by the expression upon her visitor's face; he looked as if he had swallowed something very indigestible and was wondering desperately if he ought to bolt out of the room.

"Well, I *do* think," said the second Giles Arcourt — namely, Rolande — unforgivingly, "that it was a shabby trick." Having rehearsed the scene previously, she stood in such a position that her back was to the firelight and to the single candle-sconce that lit the room, so her face was now almost completely in shadow. "But if he is willing to give it up now — What is your name? Your true name?" she addressed the visitor abruptly, in German.

The wretched youth stared up at Rolande in consternation. "I — I don't — " he stammered, clinging to the tatters of his impersonation.

"Schmidt — *nicht wahr*?" his alter ego pursued relentlessly. "Otto Schmidt? Josef Schmidt? Franz Schmidt? I myself was brought up as Johann Schmidt, and called myself so before I discovered the documents that proved to me that I was really Giles Arcourt — What is that?" she broke off to enquire rather exasperatedly, as the knocker sounded abruptly and a confused hubbub of voices immediately broke out in the hall beyond the door. "Cousin Louisa, I understood you had instructed your butler to deny you to visitors this evening!"

"So I had," said the Baroness, equally exasperated, for, like Rolande, she believed they were upon the very point of wringing a confession from Giles Arcourt. "I cannot think what — Jasper!" she exclaimed, in tones of the deepest disapproval, as Mr. Carrington, looking quite unruffled after what had ob-

135

viously been a brief, sharp, but successful altercation with Hendon, walked into the room. "What are *you* doing here?"

"I've come to enquire if you and the Countess have recovered from the excessive fatigue engendered by attending the concert this afternoon, of course," Jasper said agreeably. He nodded to Rolande, who was regarding him in open consternation. "Hullo, young Giles," he said. "I thought I told you to lie low."

"I — I — " Rolande stammered. She was furious with Jasper for having been clever enough to realise that she and the Baroness were up to something that evening, but she was also slightly intimidated by an unwonted steely gleam she saw in his eyes behind his pose of affability.

He cut her off, turning to address the bogus Giles Arcourt, who was regarding him with a terrified gaze.

"And you, my young imposter," he said pleasantly, "are you quite satisfied now that you really had best give up this preposterous farce of pretending that you are Giles Arcourt? As you can see for yourself, the genuine article has now turned up, so this Banbury tale my aunt has concocted about your origin will scarcely hold water any longer."

Giles stared at him dumbly.

"Well?" said Jasper encouragingly. "May I suggest that you make a bolt for it, halfling? Croil will scarcely have any other choice than to turn you over to the Authorities when it becomes known to them that a second and far more authentic Giles Arcourt has come on the scene, and, though I don't know precisely what the penalty is for impersonation and fraud, I seem to recall that a gentleman named John Hatfield was hanged not many years back for a crime of a similar nature. Not being of a vindictive turn of mind, I shouldn't care to see that happen to you, especially since it seems to me that Croil deserves the penalty far more than do you; hence my advice to you to lope off at once to your native land. If you are in need of funds — "

"Nein — nein!" Giles protested, his English escaping him in the agitation of the moment. He rose, gazing from one to the other of them as if quite at a loss what to say or do next, and then all at once plunged out of the room into the hall, where they heard him demanding his hat and stick from Hendon in an unintelligible mixture of German and English.

The moment the front door had closed behind him, Rolande and the Baroness fell upon Jasper.

"You have ruined everything!" Rolande exclaimed, in the greatest vexation.

The Baroness said, "Really, Jasper, this is too bad of you! I told you I did not wish to receive visitors this evening!"

"Yes, and I was quite right in believing there was something behind *that*!" Jasper said scathingly. The easy, negligent manner that he had used with Giles Arcourt had quite disappeared, and even the Baroness, a notably courageous woman, quailed slightly before the icy gaze he turned upon her. "I couldn't, however, have been expected to guess," he continued, "that even *you* would have concocted such a tottyheaded, totally skip-brained plan as this — "

"It wasn't!" said Rolande hotly. "We were on the

very point of frightening him into a confession when you ruined everything by interfering. Oh, *why* need you have come here tonight? If you knew we had a plan on foot, couldn't you have trusted us?''

''Trusted you!'' Jasper gave a short and what seemed to Rolande a very disagreeable laugh. ''I should as soon have trusted a pair of idiot children — and it seems I was quite right. I must admit, though, that I had no idea that your folly would carry you to *these* lengths! Did it never enter your head, Louisa'' he demanded, turning grimly upon the Baroness, ''that in allowing Miss Henry to resume her masquerade as Giles Arcourt, you were exposing her to a great deal of danger? How long, do you imagine, will it take Croil to put two and two together, when that boy runs to him with the tale of what has happened here tonight, and come out with the realisation that for *two* people who resemble Mrs. John Arcourt to turn up suddenly in Brighton is far too unlikely a coincidence, and that the Countess Móra and the young man the boy saw here tonight are actually one and the same person?''

The Baroness for the first time looked slightly taken aback.

''But he will not run to Croil!'' she protested, after a moment. ''He will go away — perhaps even back to Vienna. You told him yourself to do so!''

''Yes, I told him to do so — but it is far more likely that he will go to Croil instead!'' Jasper said. ''He is frightened and confused now, but when he has had a little time to think the matter over, I shouldn't care to wager a groat that he won't put his faith in Croil, rather than in his own wits, to extricate him from the bumblebath he has fallen into!" He turned again to Rolande. "No," he said, "the only safe thing to do is to get you out of Brighton before Croil has been able to devise another of his clever little plans to put you out of the way."

But this statement brought an immediate chorus of protest down upon him.

"I won't go!" Rolande declared recalcitrantly. "It is impossible! Not until I am sure that odious boy has stopped pretending to be Giles Arcourt!"

And at the same moment the Baroness remarked warmly, "Oh no, Jasper dear! You *can't* be so unfeeling! I have the distinct impression that young Lord Hoult is definitely forming an attachment for Rolande, and it would be *too* devastating if you obliged her to go away before he has come to the point of making her a declaration!"

As the Baroness's voice was more forceful than Rolande's, it was her words that Jasper heard more clearly, or at least they seemed to capture the greater part of his attention.

"A declaration!" he ejaculated, with a look of what appeared to Rolande to be irritated superiority upon his face. "Don't be absurd, Louisa! To whom is he to make this declaration? To the *Countess Móra*? And what happens when he discovers that this lady is a complete fabrication — from her name and ancestry to the colour of her hair?"

"Well, he would not be the first man to discover that he had married a *brune* instead of a *blonde*, or the other way round," said the Baroness obstinately. "And at any rate, when a man is top-over-tail in love, he doesn't care tuppence *who* the girl is. And, after all, Rolande's grandfather *was* a baronet. The Henrys are a very old family — I won't say a very respectable one, but then so few of us are."

Jasper, however, merely reiterated that she had windmills in her head if she expected young Hoult to make an offer for a girl who had been parading up and down Brighton under a false name and a mane of false hair, which statement so infuriated Rolande that she said she would show him whether Lord Hoult would make an offer for her or not, and that furthermore she would accept him when he did.

"You said the same thing about Geraint only yesterday," Jasper said dampingly, "and you have precisely as much chance of marrying *him*. Besides, if you care to go about disguised as a *femme fatale*, you will have just as good an opportunity in France as in England to snare a titled husband — rather more, I should think, as they aren't nearly so particular over there since the Revolution."

Rolande said dangerously that she was not going to France.

"Oh yes, you are," Jasper said. "You are going wherever I choose to send you. And don't you dare," he added, with equal menace in his own voice, "leave this house without my knowledge and permission. Is that understood?"

Rolande, with her chin in the air, said that she and the Baroness had been invited to the breakfast being given on the following day by Lord Hoult and Sir Robert Carlisle, and that she certainly intended to go.

"Very well, you may go," said Jasper. "I shall

escort you. And now go upstairs at once and take off those ridiculous clothes before anyone else sees you in them.''

Rolande began to remind him that it was he who had first induced her to put them on, but found herself addressing empty air, as before she had spoken two words he walked out into the hall, reclaimed his hat and stick from Hendon, and left the house.

''And it has stopped raining; he won't even get wet!'' she said vengefully, running to the window and pulling aside the curtain to see that the storm had blown over almost as quickly as it has begun. ''It would serve him much more right if he were to drown!''

''Oh no, we shouldn't care to have him drowned,'' said the Baroness, who was somewhat literal-minded, ''or there would be no point in our trying any longer to save him from being defrauded of eight million pounds. But he *is* an extraordinarily exasperating man. Sometimes it hardly appears to me that he deserves all the effort we are putting into this.''

''I shall never forgive him — never!'' declared Rolande; but whether she meant she would not forgive him for the aspersions he had cast upon her ability to make a noble match, or for his interfering with their plans, she did not make clear, and in point of fact was probably not sure herself.

TWELVE

Neither Rolande nor the Baroness had a restful night's sleep after the events of the highly upsetting evening. Both were hopeful that the appearance of a second Giles Arcourt upon the scene would have frightened the first into giving up his own impersonation and leaving Brighton, but both likewise had the uneasy feeling that Jasper might be right and that they had done something for which they would be sorry later.

In Rolande's case this feeling was complicated by the conviction that Jasper intended to send her away immediately and that she would never see him again. As she was extremely angry with him, she told herself that this would be a very good thing, but at the same time, quite contrarily, she made up her mind that nothing would induce her to leave Brighton, and that if Jasper succeeded in winning the Baroness over to his point of view and the Baroness turned her out, she would remain even if she had to go to the Castle Inn and hire herself out as a chambermaid.

As a result of their losing a good deal of sleep over these unprofitable speculations, she and the Baroness found themselves facing each other over the breakfast table at a rather advanced hour on the following morning. Rolande, who was expecting Geraint to call, had taken the trouble to allow Disbrey to make her up as the Countess Móra, and was attired in a charming morning-frock of blue-and-silver muslin, but the Baroness was still in one of her extraordinary dressing gowns, though wearing her black diamonds. She said they helped her to concentrate.

She had concentrated on nothing but a rather esoteric breakfast of angelcakes and chocolate, however, when Hendon suddenly appeared to announce Lady Prest and Mrs. Falkirk. The Baroness looked at Rolande, raised her eyebrows dramatically, and as soon as Hendon had left the room hissed at her, "Silence! Deny everything!"

Rolande nodded, her heart beginning to beat a little faster. She could not help thinking that this unexpected morning-call must have something to do with the events of the previous evening.

That she was not mistaken in this supposition was obvious the moment the visitors trod into the breakfast-parlour. Peggy Falkirk looked distressed and somewhat embarrassed, while Lady Prest had a brow like a thundercloud and a bearing so militant that Rolande was reminded of stories of Queen Elizabeth or Catherine the Great in a mood of deep royal displeasure. Lady Prest said at once to the Baroness, pointing her sunshade at her to emphasise her words, "Louisa! I want a word with you!"

"As many as you like, Honoria," said the Baroness, who had put on an extremely affable air. "Peggy, dear — how nice to see you, and looking so lovely, as you always do! You must both sit down and have some chocolate."

"No, thank you!" said Lady Prest firmly. She continued to stand rigidly erect before her cousin, regarding her with an icy gaze. "Do not," she said, "think to fob me off with this air of false hospitality, Louisa! I have come here for information, and information I intend to have!" She paused for a moment, as if for effect, and then demanded in even more impressive tones, "Where is Giles?"

"Giles?" said the Baroness innocently. "Giles?" Oh, do you mean that dreadful boy you are trying to foist on us all as poor John's son? But how should I know where he is, Honoria dear? He resides with *you*, doesn't he?"

"Yes," said Lady Prest grimly, "he resides with me, Louisa, and I may tell you — not at all to your surpise, I am sure — that he did not come home last night."

"Didn't he?" said the Baroness. "Well, I must say, my dear, that that *does* surprise me a bit, for he seems rather too young for that sort of thing. But young people are so very precocious these days."

"I do not," Lady Prest interrupted, still with her thundercloud face, "suspect him of dallying with some fast female, Louisa! What I suspect is foul play! He came here, to this house, last evening — "

"Aunt Honoria — please!" Peggy Falkirk said,

her face pink with embarrassment. "You can't believe —"

"Ah, but I can!" said Lady Prest, without removing her stern gaze from the Baroness's face. "And,
what is more, I most certainly do! Louisa, *where is that
boy*?"

"Where is your bogus Giles Arcourt? But, my dear
Honoria, how on earth should I know?" said the
Baroness, trying to sound quite bewildered, which was
rather difficult in view of the fact that she was feeling
immensely triumphant.

It was now obvious that the plan she and Rolande
had devised had succeeded perfectly, and that Giles Arcourt, terrified at the prospect of being unmasked as an
imposter, had decided that the only safe thing for him
to do was to disappear. She only wished that Jasper
were present to hear of their success, and looked forward with great pleasure to telling him all about it and
making him eat his scathing words about people who
behaved like "idiot children."

Unfortunately, it was not Jasper, but Geraint,
whom Hendon appeared at that moment to announce.
The young man came impetuously into the room,
looked with dismay upon his mama and then reproach-
fully at Peggy, and said quickly to the latter, "I thought
you would stop her from coming here!"

"I *did* try," Peggy began in a low voice, defending
herself, though with a rather frightened glance at Lady
Prest; but she got no further.

"I can only hope, Geraint," Lady Prest said, addressing her offspring with the maximum amount of

impressiveness, "that you have come here to further my efforts to discover what has happened to your unfortunate cousin. If you have not, I must request you to go away at once. It would be too upsetting, in the present unhappy state of affairs, to be faced with disloyalty in the bosom of one's own family."

Geraint coloured up and would have spoken, but he was interrupted by the Baroness.

"As it is *my* house, Honoria," she said pointedly, "I *do* think you are taking rather much on yourself by asking *my* guest to go away. Geraint, dear boy, I am very glad to see you, and of course you must not leave. Won't you sit down?"

Geraint, with a glance of mixed defiance and apprehension at his mother, said he couldn't very well, as long as she and Peggy were standing.

"Well, then, perhaps *they* will go away," the Baroness said inspirationally, "or at least Honoria will. She seems to have taken the extraordinary notion into her head that, because her young protégé paid us a call last evening, we have him immured in a closet here, or perhaps have murdered him and buried him somewhere beneath the cellar floor. Quite melodramatic, but really not the sort of thing that goes on in Brighton, Honoria dear. In Russia, now — "

"I do not wish to hear anything about Russia, Louisa!" Lady Prest interrupted inexorably, not to be deterred from the main topic by diversions. "I wish only to know what occurred at this house last evening, when that unfortunate boy was rash enough to come here alone. I must warn you," she added impressively, lifting her hand as the Baroness attempted to speak, "that I am already aware that Jasper Carrington visited this house at that time as well."

"Well, I don't see how you can be aware of that, unless you have been spying upon him," the Baroness said, in a tone of strong censure, "but I see no reason to deny it. Jasper has every right in the world to call upon any lady he likes. We had a very agreeable conversation, and he left shortly after your bogus Giles did."

"In-deed! He did not follow, I presume?"

"With murder in his heart? Really, Honoria, you have been reading too many lending-library novels!" said the Baroness. "Jasper is far too indolent to murder anyone; he has even given up duelling, he says, since it necessitates rising at such a disagreeably early hour in the morning."

"It would be very much to his advantage to have Giles put out of the way!"

"Yes, I daresay it would," said the Baroness, "but I must remind you, Honoria, that, however much you may dislike him, Jasper *is* a gentleman. *So* different from being a lady, my dear, who may do almost anything and still salve her conscience with the happy thought of how superior she is to the rest of the world. Yes — what is it, Hendon?" she enquired, as the butler once more trod discreetly into the room.

"Mr. Carrington, Madame," said Hendon, and the next moment Jasper himself walked in.

"Well, well — quite a family gathering we have here," he said, raising his brows at sight of the Baroness's guests. "Aunt Honoria — Peggy — Geraint

— '' He bowed to Rolande, who had not said a word since the visitors had arrived, partly because no one had said anything to her and partly because she was so pleased over the success of her plan to get rid of Giles Arcourt that she was afraid she would betray it if she spoke. She prudently continued to keep silent as Jasper went on, to the Baroness, ''But why are they all standing? Can it be, Cousin Louisa, that you have not made these nearest and dearest of your kith and kin welcome?''

''We have not come,'' Lady Prest said austerely, forestalling the Baroness's reply, ''upon a social call, Jasper. As you are no doubt already aware'' — she spoke these words, it seemed to her audience, with a marked degree of venom — ''your young cousin Giles has disappeared. He did not come home last night after calling upon Louisa and the Countess, and naturally we are at our wit's end to know what has become of him.''

''Naturally,'' said Jasper, casting a glance at the Baroness, who was finding it very difficult not to look smug. ''But I shouldn't worry, if I were you, Aunt Honoria. Ten to one he'll turn up sooner or later, none the worse for wear.''

''Honoria thinks it is quite probable that you have murdered him,'' the Baroness said to him helpfully. ''She has been reading too many lending-library novels, I fear. Perhaps if you would take a solemn oath of your innocence on the grave of your mother, it might soothe her. It usually seems to do so in fiction of that type.''

Jasper said that unfortunately his mother was buried in Yorkshire, and Lady Prest, in the coldest of accents, informed them that she found nothing amusing in such talk.

"I shall set Mr. Croil to work on this matter at once," she said, "and if it should develop, as I am sadly afraid it will, that a member of my family has been involved in the disappearance of this unfortunate boy, I shall do *nothing* — I repeat, *nothing* — to prevent the full rigour of the Law from being visited upon him." She was, of course, looking at Jasper as she pronounced these words, and added with some bitterness, "As I can see it will be of no use whatever to expect to obtain any further information here, I shall leave. Peggy — Geraint, do you come with us?"

Geraint stammered that he would like a word first with the Countess. Lady Prest, looking revolted, swept past him to the door, but Jasper, moving swiftly, forestalled Peggy as she was about to follow her.

"Listen to me, Peggy dear," he said to her in a low voice. "You know that matter I spoke of to you the other evening? It's more important than ever now — do you understand? If you hear Aunt Honoria and Croil making any sort of plan that involves Giles Arcourt — *or* the Countess — you must let me know at once. It's life or death. Will you promise?"

"Life or death? The Countess?" Peggy's great blue eyes, looking bewildered and a trifle frightened, raised themselves to his face. "Jasper, what *is* this about?"

"Never mind. Do you promise?"

"Oh — very well! Of course I promise."

"Good! And now off you go, my dear, before that

witch comes riding back on her broomstick to fetch you."

Rolande, who was watching the two of them, although she was pretending to be listening to Geraint as he tried at one and the same time to apologise for his mother's actions and to request her permission to escort her to the breakfast that afternoon, saw the affectionate glance that passed between Jasper and Peggy as the latter departed, and a pang of jealousy, so unexpected and painful that she felt she could hardly bear it, passed through her heart.

Being a girl of spirit, however, and being aware, besides, that Jasper had not the least interest in her beyond getting her out of Brighton as quickly as possible, she resolutely denied to herself that she had felt anything at all; but she could not prevent herself from looking so unhappy that Geraint, fearing that what he considered her delicate and sensitive nature had been seriously affected by the disagreeable scene she had just witnessed, confounded himself in apologies for his mother's behaviour.

"She is upset over what is probably only a silly boy's prank," he said, "and when she is upset she is very apt to say things she doesn't mean. But you *will* allow me to escort you, Countess — ?"

The Countess said that, unfortunately, Mr. Carrington had already claimed that privilege, and that, furthermore, it did not appear to her that he was in a mood this morning to be persuaded to give it up. This, as Geraint could see for himself, was quite true; Jasper, now that Lady Prest and Peggy had gone, was looking at him in a way that plainly indicated he was waiting with some impatience for his departure as well. Geraint, accustomed to accommodating his autocratic cousin in all his wishes, reluctantly took his leave, and Jasper, closing the door behind him, at once turned with considerably acerbity to the Baroness.

"I hope, Louisa," he said to her, "you are pleased with this hornets' nest you have stirred up!"

The Baroness looked at him with some astonishment. "Well, yes, I am!" she said candidly. "Don't you understand, dear boy? We have won the game; Honoria has been romped —"

"Does it appear so to you?" Jasper asked grimly. "You are very sanguine! To me, on the contrary, it seems that my aunt Honoria has now had every suspicion she ever had of the Countess confirmed — or didn't you see the way she was looking at her, though she didn't deign to address a word to her? — and that she means both to get that wretched young moonling of hers back and to see to it that *our* Giles Arcourt disappears in his place. Good God, Louisa, you know Croil will be able to trace that boy without the least trouble! He'll have him back here within four-and-twenty hours — *and* the whole story of the copper-haired youth who was produced in this house while the raven-haired Countess was conveniently unable to appear because of — what excuse did the two of you think up for that? A migraine? How uninventive! At any rate, it is obvious that we shall have to get Miss Henry out of Brighton as soon as I can complete the arrangements — and in the meanwhile, she is not to stir from this house except under my escort! I hope that is well understood!"

The Baroness, looking somewhat taken aback at

this ruthless destruction of her happy illusions of triumph, nevertheless stubbornly clung to her guns and remarked dampingly that she believed he was making a great to-do over nothing.

"To hear you talk, one would think Croil was one of those genies who spring out of bottles at people and perform the most impossible tasks for them," she said. "*I* think the boy has disappeared for good, and I am quite certain that, even if Croil *does* succeed in finding him, he will be far too frightened to take up his role as Giles Arcourt again. Which means that it is *quite* safe for Rolande to remain in Brighton and continue to fascinate young Hoult, because, even if Honoria *has* guessed that the Countess Móra is your Giles Arcourt, it can't make a ha'porth of difference to her now whether *he* inherits the Arcourt fortune or *you* do, since she has lost her own Giles and is therefore quite out of the running."

Jasper, however, looked unconvinced, and, merely remarking that, as always, her thinking revealed her as an incurable widgeon, said he had matters to attend to and went off, promising — or rather threatening, as the Baroness put it — to return again by half after two.

THIRTEEN

He reappeared precisely at that hour, driving his curricle and bringing with him old General Pusey, who was driving a barouche. Jasper coolly explained that, as the curricle would not comfortably accommodate three, he had asked the General to take the Baroness up in his barouche — an arrangement which was obviously extremely satisfactory to the General. The Baroness, who knew it was quite useless to argue with Jasper when he was in this mood, gave him a dagger-glance but allowed herself to be led off in triumph by the General, while Rolande mounted into the curricle with Jasper.

She was looking exceedingly smart that afternoon in a gown of marigold yellow and a pebble necklace and earrings, but she could scarcely flatter herself that she was making any impression upon Jasper, who gave her only a cursory glance as he helped her up into the curricle and then seemed to forget about her altogether, devoting all his attention to the managing of his team of splendid chestnuts, who seemed very fresh and on the fret, in spite of the warmth of the afternoon.

Rolande, who was determined not to sit silent like a chidden schoolgirl during the drive, asked after a brief time, as the curricle drove out of the Steyne and up on to the East Cliff, how far it was to the farm where Lord Hoult and Sir Robert had arranged to give their *déjeuner champêtre*.

"It's not far from Shoreham — a matter of less than ten miles from here," Jasper said, glancing over at her with a slight and, she considered, rather sardonic lift of his eyebrows. "You won't be obliged," he continued unexpectedly, "to endure my company for long."

Rolande was very much taken aback. She had been so busy trying to conquer her own feelings and prevent Jasper from realising that she was quite disgracefully in love with him that it had never occurred to her up to this time to wonder what he was making of her behaviour towards him; and it therefore came as a good deal of a shock to her now to find that, far from suspecting that she cared for him, he was convinced that she genuinely disliked him.

"*C'est affreux*, this is dreadful!" she said to herself in great dejection. But it was only a moment before she realised that, far from being dreadful, the situation was exactly what was most to be desired if one was cast, as she undoubtedly was, in the role of a despised and rejected female. At least it left one with one's pride intact.

So she chattered away indefatigably to Jasper as they drove through the hot, still afternoon, avoiding the vexed subject of her future and behaving like any young lady of fashion who was being escorted to a modish social function and had no other thought on her mind but to enjoy herself.

"No doubt he thinks me excessively silly," she thought, as Jasper failed to respond to what she herself admitted was one of her more unsuccessful sallies; but to say the truth Jasper appeared to be preoccupied with other thoughts, and would no doubt not have responded suitably even if she had been dropping pearls of wisdom and wit for his benefit.

When they arrived at the farm where the breakfast was to be held they were met at the end of a winding lane by Lord Hoult and Sir Robert, each of whom presented Rolande with an elegant bouquet. She and Jasper were then directed to an expanse of emerald greensward where several large tents of white and rose-coloured muslin had been set up, and which was already thronged with a fashionable crowd, strolling about in the shade of thick shrubberies hung with garlands of fresh flowers. They were to dine in the tents to the sound of the village bells, and there would be dancing and games, a display of fireworks, and even a Maypole decorated with garlands and ribands for such of the guests to prance around, Jasper said, as cared to imagine themselves as rustic swains and maidens.

Rolande, noting that he spoke in a disparaging tone, perversely said that she would enjoy of all things dancing round a Maypole, and was encouraged in this desire by Lord Hoult, who, as soon as he had greeted the last of his arriving guests, at once rushed to her side and enthusiastically offered to partner her. Owing to his maladroitness, however — for he had no eyes for anyone but her and paid very little serious attention to the tricky business of managing his riband — their ribands soon became inextricably entangled, putting everyone else out and drawing from Jasper, who was standing comfortably leaning against a tree watching them, a look of bored amusement that made Rolande want to hit him.

But she was back at her old hopeless admiration again when, targets having been set up and bows and arrows brought for those guests who wished to indulge in the rustic sport of archery, she saw him easily best the most expert of his competitors, sending shaft after shaft to pierce the mark. He had stripped off his coat, and stood, a perfect Adonis, she thought, in shirt and tight-fitting breeches, in silhouette against the greenery behind him, his fair hair ruffled by the breeze, his face calm, but with an unwonted expression of concentration upon it as he set himself to let the arrow fly once more at the mark.

"*Qu'il est beau!*" she thought, and looked in despair at Lord Hoult's eager, commonplace young face beside her. Could it be, she asked herself with a melancholy sigh, that there was no choice for her but to become Lady Hoult or to return to her distasteful life in the French provincial theatre? It was true, there was always Geraint, but he was Jasper's cousin, and if she married him she would be bound to see more of Jasper than she felt she could bear.

As if in response to her thought of him, Geraint suddenly appeared at her side, looking oddly warm and harassed, it seemed to her.

"Thank God I have found you!" he said to her at once, in a low, urgent voice. "I must speak to you alone, Countess! It is a matter of the utmost importance!"

"Of the utmost importance?"

Rolande stared at him a trifle doubtfully. His face certainly wore an expression of intense gravity, and she wondered if it was because he had come to the determination, in spite of his mother, to make her an offer. A crowded fête seemed a rather odd setting to choose for a declaration, but she dared say he might feel that it would be an easy matter for them to wander off together somewhere into the shrubberies without being missed.

The problem was that she was not at all sure that she wished him to make her an offer now; in fact, she was almost certain that she did not. Things were too unsettled; one always went on hoping, even when one knew there were no logical grounds for hope; and, to put matters on the most practical plane, this was assuredly not the time and place to inform him that the lady to whom he was offering marriage was not the "Countess Móra," but an impecunious young actress named Rolande Henry.

It would be expedient, therefore, she thought, to temporise — a matter that presented no immediate difficulties, for on her other side Lord Hoult was making jealous efforts to regain her attention, while Jasper, laying down his bow and resuming his coat, came over at once to join them. He had obviously decided, she saw, to put a few more touches on his *grande passion* role, and, emulating Lord Hoult's behaviour, stared coldly at Geraint and then began to look at her — as he himself had once expressed it — like a dog regarding a particularly delicious bone. She was quite indignant with him, and, suddenly reversing her intentions, walked off with Geraint, hanging conspicuously upon his arm.

To her annoyance — and to Geraint's serious displeasure, she saw — Jasper followed them.

"Going for a turn about the grounds?" he said affably. "An excellent idea! I shall join you."

Geraint looked at him, compressing his lips. It occurred to Rolande that he was regarding Jasper in a peculiarly unfriendly manner, which was not at all like him, for his admiration for his dashing cousin was ordinarily quite uncritical. She dared say, however, that jealousy was at the root of it.

"I should think," he suggested austerely after a moment to Jasper, "that after your exercise you would prefer having a glass of iced moselle or champagne in the shade."

"Not a bit of it," said Jasper cheerfully. "A stroll is exactly what I should like best." He looked at his cousin, upon whose face a rather high flush had now arisen. "In point of fact," he said with an air of solicitude, "you look as if you could do with a cool, soothing drink yourself, coz. Are you sure you wouldn't care to have me take the Countess off your hands while you go back to the refreshment tent?"

Geraint said with some heat that he considered the opportunity of a conversation with the Countess the greatest of privileges, which he would not forgo for any reason.

"Oh, come now," said Jasper. "*I* can think of a number of reasons."

Geraint said that he did not wish to hear any of them, and again suggested, not very subtly, that his cousin return to the fête and leave him and Rolande alone.

Jasper pretended to look shocked. "No, no. — couldn't think of *that*, dear boy!" he said. "Come to think of it, not at all the thing for the Countess to be wandering off into the shrubbery with either of us — her exalted position and all that, you know. Much better if we all go back and join the others — don't you agree?"

Geraint, obviously realising by this time that it was quite impossible for him to get rid of his cousin, gave up the idea of a tête-à-tête in despair and assented. They all returned, therefore, to the area where the tents had been set up, and not long afterwards a few loud, imperative blasts of a trumpet announced that dinner was to be served.

Geraint, of course, made a determined effort to seat himself beside Rolande, but found himself out-jockeyed by Jasper and Lord Hoult, who, being less scrupulous about displaying good manners, managed to take their places one on each side of her, leaving Geraint the poor consolation of sitting opposite her and gloomily watching as they took it in turns to converse with her.

When the sumptuous — and, to him, interminable — meal was over, he darted at once to her side. But he was again too late to get her to himself as she was led off by Jasper and young Lord Hoult through an archway of roses hung with gaily coloured lanterns (it was by this time growing quite dark) to another tent, where several of the most celebrated performers from the Italian Opera were about to give a concert. The Baroness, who had been watching with some interest the little three-sided chess game he, Jasper, and Lord Hoult had been engaging in, in their efforts to capture the Countess's attention, felt with some satisfaction that, if anything more was needed to bring Lord Hoult to the point, this should certainly do it, and made her own effort to draw Jasper off and allow young Hoult a clear field. This she did by sitting next to her cousin at the concert and using the same tactics that had been so successful at Promenade Grove in engrossing Geraint's attention and thus permitting Rolande and Giles Arcourt to go off alone there.

This time, however, they were quite *unsuccessful.*

"I know what you want," Jasper said to her when, at the concert's end, she had brilliantly managed so to entangle her long topaz necklace in her gauzy pelerine that it was quite impossible for her to extricate herself without assistance. "You want General Pusey. He has never been in the Navy, of course, but I understand he considers himself an expert on knots. He's asleep over there in the corner. I'll send him to you directly."

And, offering his arm to the Countess Móra, he walked off with her, leaving the Baroness speechless with frustration and still as inextricably entangled as ever.

By this time Geraint had quite despaired of being able to manage a private conversation with the Countess, and, seizing upon one of the servants, all of whom, in the spirit of this *fête champêtre*, had been picturesquely disguised as gardeners in smocks and were therefore not their usual efficient selves, demanded pen, ink, and paper of him. His request was a good while in being gratified, and in the interim he was entertained by a splendid display of fireworks, which the Countess, of course, was enjoying in the company of Jasper and Lord Hoult.

When at last the desired items had been brought to him, he wrote hastily, without salutation or preamble, "You are in the greatest danger! Beware of my cousin Jasper! Do not under any circumstances allow yourself to be alone with him! I beg you to place yourself under my protection! Prest."

Having read this missive over, he wished he had not used quite so many exclamation points; but it was now growing late and at any moment, he felt, the Countess might be lured into Jasper's curricle for the return journey to Brighton. He had discovered from the Baroness that that was how she had come, and had represented to her the impropriety of allowing the Countess to drive about the countryside at night alone in an open carriage with a man; but the Baroness had only said that, as she and the General would be directly behind the curricle in their barouche all the way, the Countess could scarcely be said to be alone with anyone. And at any rate, she had added, the Countess might go in the barouche with her and the General if she chose.

The carefully folded note was put into Rolande's hand just as the exhibition of fireworks was coming to an end.

"What is that?" enquired Jasper, who always saw everything that was going on, and had no scruples about asking awkward questions.

Rolande, who was trying to decipher the note in the moonlight — for the lanterns that had been earlier hung on trees and shrubs to provide a convenient amount of illumination had almost all been extinguished when the fireworks had begun — said she couldn't quite make it out, but she suspected it was from Lord Prest.

"Well, I daresay it will keep until we are back in Brighton," Jasper said. "I don't see why he need write notes to you, at any rate; he is standing just over there, and could say anything he liked to you if he would take the pains to walk twenty paces. Shall we be going now, Countess? You will enjoy the drive back to Brighton in the moonlight, I believe."

Rolande, who was still puzzling over the note, but could make out little beyond Jasper's name and so concluded it could not be an offer of marriage, put it into her reticule and said she was quite ready to go. The Baroness and General Pusey were collected, adieux were said and compliments paid to their two young hosts, and in a very few minutes, to Geraint's horror, Jasper was helping Rolande up into his curricle.

The drive to Brighton indeed promised, as Jasper had said, to be an agreeable one. The moon was up in a cloudless, dark-sapphire sky; the air was warm and still; and Rolande, flushed with the triumph of having had no fewer than three young men pursuing her relentlessly all day, was in a far happier mood than she had been in some hours before, during the drive from Brighton.

She was wondering if any of Jasper's persistence in remaining beside her during the whole of the fête could be attributed to genuine inclination rather than to a sense of duty when she was suddenly puzzled to find the curricle, which had just rounded a curve in the road, turning into a narrow, tree-shadowed lane instead of continuing on its way upon the high road.

"What are you doing? Why are you turning in here?" she enquired curiously.

For reply, Jasper merely shook his head and enjoined silence upon her by putting his finger to his lips. He had halted his horses just out of sight of the road, but she could hear the barouche, which had fallen slightly behind them, also come round the curve in the high road and go steadily on, apparently in the belief that the curricle was still proceeding on before it. A thousand conjectures raced through Rolande's mind in a moment, the chief of them dealing with the possibility that Jasper might really be in love with her, and had contrived this ruse to be alone with her here in this secluded spot.

The next moment, however, this exciting and, on the whole, pleasurable supposition was rudely removed from the realm of possibility when Jasper calmly turned the curricle and, driving out of the lane, set off in the direction from which they had just come.

"What *are* you doing?" Rolande demanded again, her puzzlement now mingled with a growing sense of suspicion and indignation. She did not trust Jasper, and his present behaviour appeared to be entirely justifying her lack of confidence in him. "We have just come from this way. Why are we going back?"

Jasper said carelessly that she would find that out soon enough, and whipped up his team so that the curricle flew along the moonlit road at an accelerated pace.

"I want to know now," Rolande said, in a strictly controlled voice that did not quite conceal the fact, however, that she was growing seriously angry. *"Sur-le-champ!* Where are we going?"

"Oh, very well," said Jasper, featheredging a corner at high speed with great skill and aplomb. "If you must know, we are going to Shoreham."

"To Shoreham? But why? Why should we go there at this time of night?"

"Well, it was the best time I could think of to abduct you," Jasper said apologetically. "I'm a bit new at this sort of thing, you see — "

But he got no further.

"To abduct me!" Rolande gasped. "To — What on earth do you mean? Why should you wish to abduct me?"

"Oh, I don't *wish* to," Jasper assured her. "Personally, it would suit me far better if you'd come along willingly; but as far as I've been able to see, there isn't much chance of that. You've never seemed in the least in the mood to co-operate whenever I've mentioned getting you out of Brighton, and I finally came to the conclusion that an abduction was the only feasible method of operation. It's a rather small yacht," he added, again apologetically, "but after all it is only a short journey to Calais. I expect you won't be too uncomfortable."

Rolande, who had been rendered almost speechless by the shock of these disclosures, had some difficulty now in arranging her thoughts into coherent speech.

"To — to *Calais*!" she managed to sputter at last. "Do you mean you intend to take me *there*? But you can't! I won't go!"

"Now, now," Jasper said soothingly, "don't be difficult, Miss Henry. Think how much more agreeable it is to be alive, even in Calais, than it is to be dead. And you needn't remain there, you know; in fact, it is my intention to take you at once to Avignon, where you will be the guest for a time of my great-aunt, a French lady who lives very retired in the country — "

"I won't go!" Rolande repeated, between shut teeth. She was very angry with Jasper, the more so because for one rapturous moment, when he had said he was abducting her, she had believed he meant that he was eloping with her. "Take me back to Brighton at once!" she commanded him. He drove on at the same breakneck pace. "Or I shall jump out of the carriage!" she added dangerously.

"Well, I should hardly advise that," Jasper said judicially. "You might break a leg, or even your neck."

Rolande, who was quite aware of this, forbore to argue the point, and after a moment said in an icy voice that he might succeed in carrying her to Shoreham, but, once there, she would certainly make an outcry and bring someone to her aid.

"Not if you're unconscious, you won't," Jasper said cheerfully. "Dear Miss Henry, I have never yet laid a hand on a female in anger, but may I point out to you that I am considered one of the finest amateur pugilists in England, and that with a single well-aimed blow to the point of the jaw I can render you quite incapable of either speech or movement for a considerable length of

165

time. And, much as I should regret being obliged to act in such an unchivalrous manner, I can assure you that it is exactly what I shall do if you look like giving me any trouble. You wouldn't care to give me your word now that you won't make a fuss before I take you aboard the *Swallow*, would you? It's pretty much of a moot point, at any rate, as it's not likely there'll be anyone about there at this hour.''

Rolande said with dignity that it was a well-known legal doctrine that promises exacted under duress were not binding, but, observing what she considered a highly unreliable glint in his eyes as he glanced briefly over at her, hastily said that it would be unnecessary for him to proceed to such drastic measures to keep her quiet.

"Good!" he said. "I shall rely upon you to be sensible, Miss Henry.''

"It is not being sensible; it is being coerced!" Rolande said bitterly. "You are ruining my life, and I shall never forgive you for it — not even if you were to beg me on your bended knees!''

"Well, I don't think I shall do that,'' Jasper said, "but one never knows. And I'm extremely sorry if I am ruining your life, Miss Henry, but in my opinion it is far better to have a ruined life than no life at all.'' The light tone disappeared from his voice; he said after a moment, rather brusquely, "If young Hoult is genuinely attached to you, he will find the means to see you again when all this has blown over. I shall make it my business to give him your direction.''

Rolande would have liked to tell him that it made not the slightest difference to her whether she ever saw

Lord Hoult again or not, but she was so angry that she felt she could not hope to speak coherently at the moment either in French or in English. So she remained silent, and in a very short time the upper town of New Shoreham — only a few points of light in the darkness at this hour — came into view, and down the steep road they went to the jetty and the black, gently rolling water below.

FOURTEEN

A small two-masted yacht, fore-and-aft rigged, was lying at anchor, and it was towards this vessel that Jasper, having left his team in the care of the solitary figure they met — a sleepy and, to Rolande's disgusted realisation, obviously half-drunken loiterer with a vaguely nautical air — directed their steps. As Jasper had pointed out to her, it would do her very little good to make an outcry here, even had she been inclined to do so, which she was not, being quite aware that if she did obtain help it could only be at the price of a frightful scandal, which would undoubtedly put an end to the Countess Móra's stay in Brighton no matter what else came of it.

So she accompanied Jasper in a simmering state of violent disapproval down the gangway on to the deck of the yacht, where he picked up a lantern that had been left burning there and led her down a steep companionway to the lower deck. Here she was invited to enter a small cabin. She did so reluctantly, hissing fiercely at

Jasper as she walked inside, "You will be sorry for this!"

"Don't be melodramatic, Miss Henry," said her infuriating captor. "I don't think I shall be sorry in the least; on the contrary, when I have you safe on foreign shores I shall probably leap for joy, as the poets say, though I must confess I have never seen anyone do it myself." He glanced about the cabin. "Will you be quite comfortable here? I shall be obliged to lock you in, you know."

Rolande said vengefully that she expected she would be frightfully *un*comfortable. "And if it comes to that," she said, "what about my clothes? I can't go jauntering all over France in these."

"All taken care of," Jasper said, pointing to a portmanteau reposing in one corner of the cabin. "I have been nothing if not thorough, you see."

"And I daresay you have left a note for the Baroness, telling her what you are doing?"

"But of course," said Jasper, and with a polite bow, he walked out of the cabin, closing and locking the door behind him.

There had been no one in sight as they had boarded the yacht, but Rolande heard the sound of voices — Jasper's and another, obviously male — when he had left her. Then silence fell once more, except for the small, restless, creaking noises a boat makes when it is lying in the water. Rolande, still boiling with anger, could not bring herself to sit down quietly, but began pacing up and down the narrow cabin, trying to think how she might escape. At first glance, it appeared to be a hopeless endeavour. The door, when she examined it, seemed to be a stout one, and the lock was quite secure. But several hours, she thought, would probably elapse before the yacht could sail with the tide, and in the meanwhile she might manage to formulate some plan.

At the present time it occurred to her that she might at least try calling for help, in case Jasper had gone off and the man to whom he had been talking turned out to be kindly disposed towards a damsel in distress. So she stood in the centre of the cabin and, throwing back her head, cried as loudly as she could, "Help! Help! Murder! Fire!"

She felt extremely silly as she did this, as she was obviously in no real peril and thus was obliged to enact this melodramatic scene in cold blood, as it were. A discouraging silence followed. She tried again, with an equal lack of success.

Frustrated, she was about to sit down upon the bunk and try to think of something else, when a sudden eruption of noise upon the deck above made her lift her head hopefully. A scuffle of some sort seemed to be in progress there; she could hear the sound of stamping footsteps and fierce, panting masculine voices. Then, abruptly, silence descended. She ran to the door and listened. Footsteps were approaching, coming down the companionway; she could again hear masculine voices, but now engaged in apparently amicable conversation.

"Help! Help! Murder! Fire!" she screamed, hope giving her cries a conviction that they had not carried when she had first tried uttering them.

To her complete astonishment, the agitated voice that answered her was Geraint's.

"Countess?" he said. "Thank God, it *is* you!

Never fear; you are quite safe now! We shall have you out in a moment!'' She heard him then, on a different note, addressing the person who had accompanied him down the companionway. "Hurry up — can't you? Look — give me the key and I'll let the lady out first; *then* you can lock the door again and break it down.''

Rolande, perfectly bewildered by this peculiar bit of conversation, heard a key turn in the lock; the next moment Geraint had rushed into the room and, apparently overcome by his joy at finding her unharmed, had seized her in his arms. She had time to notice, in the fleeting moment before she was swept into his embrace, that he looked rather dishevelled and that his right eye was quite swollen and already half closed.

"My poor angel!'' he said thickly.

Rolande, sensing rather than actually seeing that there was someone else in the cabin, peered cautiously over his shoulder and observed that a thickset man with a thatch of grey curls was regarding them tolerantly from the doorway.

"Now you want to give over the billing and cooing, my sonny, '' he said, in an avuncular tone, '' 'cos my guv'nor he'll likely be back in a brace of snaps, and 'twon't do to have him find you here — nor the lady, neither, not with this door looking the way it does. You lope off now, and I'll see to it that all's shipshape by the time he gets here.'' He looked impersonally at the door. "I think an axe will do it,'' he said. '' 'Tis a pity you couldn't have drawn my claret when we had our little turn-up on deck; 'twould have made it all look more nat'ral-like. But I dessay I can tell him you held a pistol to my head.''

171

Rolande, having extricated herself from Geraint's embrace, and feeling by this time that she had certainly gone mad, or else that the others had, said that no doubt it was very stupid of her, but she could not quite understand why it was necessary to break down the door when she was already free.

"Well, you see," said Geraint, looking slightly embarrassed, "it's so this fellow won't be obliged to tell Jasper that he let me have the key. It will be much better if it looks as if I overpowered him and then broke down the door — "

Rolande, regarding Geraint's slim figure and the powerful one of the burly individual standing in the doorway, thought that it would take more than a broken door to make Jasper swallow *that* story; but she honoured Geraint for obviously having at least made the endeavour to rescue her by force before he had realised that bribery was a more effective means, and smiled upon him very kindly.

"Well, I do not care what Mr. Carrington thinks," she said, "but I am very grateful to you for rescuing me. And now will you take me back to Brighton, please, before he returns?"

For she placed no reliance at all upon Geraint's being able to overpower Jasper and succeed in removing her from the yacht, were her abductor to reappear.

Geraint, though still obviously quite above himself because of his unqualified success in the role of knight-errant, agreed that at the moment discretion was the better part of valour, and escorted her tenderly up the companionway. As she reached the deck, she saw that Jasper's curricle had disappeared, and that the loiterer in whose charge it had been left was now guarding a smart phaeton. He stared and scratched his head as Geraint escorted Rolande from the *Swallow* and helped her mount into this vehicle, but accepted the coin Geraint tossed to him with no more comment than a leering grin.

"How," Rolande demanded, as Geraint sprang up beside her and gave his horses the office to start, "did you know I was here? Did you follow us from the fête? I *do* think you have been terribly clever!"

Geraint said modestly that it had really all been Peggy's doing.

"Peggy?" Rolande stared. "Do you mean Mrs. Falkirk? But what can she possibly have had to do with it? She was not at the breakfast — was she?"

"Oh, no — but she had warned me beforehand, you see, of what was likely to happen." He went on, seeing that Rolande was still looking quite bewilderd, "She came to me in a great taking just as I was leaving the house, and said she had overheard Croil talking to Mama, and feared, from the few words she had been able to understand, that there was some sort of plot on foot to spirit you away from Brighton tonight on board a boat. She begged me to tell Jasper about it — well, you know I am very fond of Peggy, but there *are* times when she has more hair than wit! I think she was of the opinion that *he* might protect you! Of course I knew at once that she had got hold of the wrong end of the stick entirely, and that it was Jasper who was planning to do the abducting: why else should he have bought that yacht? I *tried* to give you warning of him during the fête," he added, looking at her rather accusingly, "but

173

I couldn't manage to get you away from him. So I finally wrote you a note — "

"Yes, I know. I didn't read it," Rolande said guiltily. "I have it here in my reticule; I thought I would read it when I was back in Brighton."

Geraint, charitably overlooking this act of dereliction of duty, went on explaining to her how he had meant to follow her when she had left the fête with Jasper in the latter's curricle, but, owing to the ill chance of his phaeton's having been blocked by other vehicles when he had endeavoured to leave, he had unfortunately been unable to do so.

"Of course I knew his yacht was lying here at Shoreham, though," he said, "so I had no difficulty in knowing where to go. I came along as soon as I could. Where is Jasper now — have you any notion? That fellow on the yacht only said he had gone off somewhere."

Rolande said she had not the least idea, adding, with more candour than tact, "But it was very foolhardy of you to have come aboard the yacht if you did not know he had gone — wasn't it? You could not possibly have hoped to overpower *him*."

Geraint, however, who had no illusions on the subject, failed to take offence at this piece of frank speaking.

"Oh yes, that is quite true," he said. "There is no one so good in a mill as Jasper. But, you see, I took the precaution of slipping one of my duelling pistols into my pocket before I left the house."

He spoke with studied carelessness, as if the fact that he should possess a pair of duelling pistols was a matter quite to be taken for granted, although it was actually the deepest of secrets between himself and their maker, Mr. Joseph Manton, since he knew very well that if his mother ever learned that he had them she would leave him no peace until he got rid of them.

"But if you had a pistol," Rolande said, puzzling the matter out, "why didn't you use it to make that man on the yacht give you the key to the cabin, instead of fighting with him?"

"Well, I did *try* to," Geraint confessed ingenuously. "But, you see — he took it away from me."

Rolande suppressed an unworthy inclination to giggle. It was so like Geraint, she thought, to allow himself, even with the advantage of a pistol, to be overmastered by the burly man.

A more sobering thought, however, soon entered her mind and drove every vestige of mirth from it. Geraint might be of the opinion that the plot to kidnap her that Peggy had overheard being discussed by Croil and Lady Prest had been hatched by Jasper, but it was far more likely, she thought — especially in view of the fact that Mrs. Falkirk herself obviously did not believe that Jasper was involved in the scheme — that it had been one of Croil's making.

In that case, it was evident that Jasper had been right in believing that the wily Croil and Lady Prest had by now realised that the Countess Móra and the copper-haired youth who so greatly resembled the late Mrs. John Arcourt were one and the same person, and that they intended mischief towards her — or, as they would think, towards *him*. And it was suddenly borne in upon her that perhaps Jasper had been quite right in considering that she had best be removed from Brighton to a place of safety, and that if she were wise she would request Geraint to turn around at once and take her back to the yacht.

To tell a man who thinks he has just rescued you from a fate worse than death that he would have done far better to leave you where you were presents certain difficulties, however, and Rolande was considering how she could best phrase her request when she was horrified to hear Geraint say, in his gravest tones, "Of course I shall not allow Jasper to go unchastised for the insult he has done you, Countess. You may rest assured of that. He may be my cousin, but in such a matter as this, blood counts for nothing."

Rolande stared at him in sudden vivid dismay. "Oh, dear!" she said. "You *don't* mean you will feel obliged to call him out?"

Geraint said rather grandiloquently that that was not the sort of matter one discussed with females.

"Oh, *mon Dieu*!" said Rolande, suddenly so exasperated with him that she could have shaken him. "*Quelle étourderie*! He will kill you, you know! And, besides, he has not done me any insult. He was only trying to save me."

"To save you!" It was now Geraint's turn to stare. "I don't understand!" he ejaculated. "How can you say such a thing when it was obviously his intention to carry you off — ?"

"Yes, but only to get me out of the country, where I would be safe!"

Rolande looked in despair at Geraint, in whose bewildered mind sudden dark vistas of international intrigue had begun to open, so that he felt the world turning topsy-turvy around him and neglected his horses to the extent that they almost bolted.

When he had them under control again, he said, in a tone of respectful awe, "Do you mean, perhaps, Countess, that you are in danger from someone hired by a foreign power — ?"

"Oh, *don't* be so stupid!" Rolande interrupted him. She was suddenly so confused by everything that had happened and by her doubts as to what she was to do now that she felt near to tears and quite incapable of keeping up the pretence any longer of being the mysterious Countess Móra. "I'm not a countess at all," she said, " and certainly not one of Royal blood! And I'm not Hungarian, either; I am half French and half English, and I am an actress named Rolande Henry. And I think that the best thing you can possibly do now is to drive me straight back to the yacht so that Mr. Carrington can take me to France!"

If the world had turned topsy-turvy for Geraint a few moments before, it now began behaving in an even more eccentric fashion, waltzing and curvetting about him so that he felt obliged to halt his horses altogether in order to concentrate upon settling it down again. That the Countess Móra was not really the Countess Móra it was not difficult for him to believe; everyone in Brighton had been convinced since she had first appeared in town that that was not her real name and rank, and had been speculating wildly upon what more exalted identity the name concealed.

But that the mysterious Countess was merely an actress, and that she had a secret connexion with his

177

cousin Jasper that had placed her in some danger from which Jasper had been attempting to rescue her — these were concepts so far beyond the scope of any of his previous imaginings that he could only stare in stunned bewilderment into Rolande's flushed, desperate face.

What he would finally have found to say to her was never to be known, however, for at that moment a closed carriage suddenly swept into view, coming from the direction of Brighton, and, upon sight of the phaeton standing motionless in the road, was pulled up sharply by its driver. While Geraint and Rolande watched in total amazement, several men sprang down and ran to the phaeton. Two of them were brandishing pistols.

"Hold them horses, Jem!" one, who appeared to be the leader, commanded; and another of the men ran immediately to carry out his bidding. The leader himself also approached the phaeton, and, seizing upon Rolande, pulled her down to the road in spite of her vigorous resistance.

This at once galvanised Geraint into activity. He launched himself from his seat to an attack upon the man below, but the outcome of this battle was never in doubt. While a third man held the struggling Rolande, the leader quickly disposed of Geraint with a blow of this pistol butt, and the young peer fell heavily to the ground.

"All right, now!" said the leader, with satisfaction. "Get him into the sack, boys!"

Rolande, of course, thought that he was referring to Geraint, and in the midst of her struggle wondered wildly why they should wish to do such a peculiar thing to him, but in a moment she saw that it was not Geraint the gang were regarding, but herself. The man who was holding her was looking at her rather dubiously, but the leader, approaching her, in a moment snatched off her hat and wig, revealing "Giles Arcourt's" close-cropped dark-copper curls.

"Didn't I tell you it warn't no female?" he demanded contemptuously. "Get him into that sack, I tell you, afore someone comes along the road!"

A large sack was produced by the man who had held Geraint's team; in a moment Rolande, still vainly resisting, had been pushed inside it. The next instant she was thrown onto the seat of the carriage; her abductors crowded in beside her; and the carriage went rattling off at breakneck speed down the deserted road under the moonlit sky.

FIFTEEN

When Geraint came to himself, he was lying peacefully in the middle of the road, with the moon beaming serenely down upon him from the cloudless sky. For a few moments he could not remember where he was or how he had got there; but recollection of the night's events soon rushed back into his mind, and he staggered hastily, albeit somewhat dizzily, to his feet.

The road was perfectly empty; there was no sign of his horses, which had undoubtedly bolted with the phaeton; and of course the closed carriage and the men who had attacked him and Rolande had long since disappeared. There was a large lump on his head and he felt very sick. But it was his duty and his intention to rescue the lady who had been under his protection, whether she was countess or actress, and with this purpose in mind he began stumbling along the road, seeking some habitation where he might find help.

He had not gone very far before there was the sound of racing hoof-beats on the road, and he was obliged to step hastily off onto the grassy verge in order to avoid being run down by a curricle that came at top speed over a rise in the road. He had time, however, to recognise the driver.

"Jasper!" he shouted, though his voice came out more in a sort of croak.

It appeared that Jasper had either heard him or seen him, however, for the curricle was immediately halted and turned about. Geraint staggered up to it.

"The Countess —" he gasped.

"Yes — what about the Countess?" Jasper said sharply. He reached down a hand to help Geraint up into the curricle. "Where is she? Good Lord!" he broke off to exclaim, as he saw his cousin's face in the moonlight. Blood had trickled freely down it from the cut on his head inflicted by the pistol butt; he presented a rather ghastly sight. "What's happened to you?" demanded Jasper.

Geraint, collapsing gratefully upon the seat, said unsteadily that he and the Countess had been set upon by a gang of men as he had been driving her back to Brighton in his phaeton.

"They knocked me unconscious, and then they must have carried her off," he said piteously. "Oh, Jasper, what are we to do? I haven't the least notion where they have taken her! It is all my fault!"

Jasper said brutally that he was quite sure of that. He seemed to be in a white rage — a condition in which Geraint had scarcely ever seen him before — and little inclined for sympathy or even civility towards his injured cousin.

"Of course," he went on acidly, "it was you who

bribed that fellow to let you take the Countess from my yacht; I gathered as much from his description of you! She would have been perfectly safe if you had left her there; as it is, God knows how we are to set about finding her! Have you no clew as to the intentions of those men who carried her off?''

Geraint said miserably that he hadn't. They had appeared out of the blue in a closed carriage, he said; there had been three or four of them; and he had been unconscious when they had driven off with the Countess.

"One of them was called Jem," he offered, not very helpfully.

Jasper said he recalled passing such a vehicle on the road, driving recklessly fast.

"But that still doesn't tell me where they are taking her," he said. He pushed his hat back on his head and sat frowning for a few moments; he appeared to be thinking. Suddenly he enquired of Geraint, "How did you know that I had taken the Countess to my yacht? You weren't following us; I made sure of that.''

"No," said Geraint. "It was Peggy."

"Peggy?"

Geraint explained briefly, as he had to Rolande, how Mrs. Falkirk had entrusted to him a message for Jasper relaying the conversation she had overheard between Croil and Lady Prest, and how he, Geraint, had deduced from it that it was Jasper himself who intended to spirit Rolande away by sea and had therefore — knowing that Jasper's yacht was lying at Shoreham — driven there as soon as he had been able to leave the fête.

"God give me patience!" Jasper exclaimed, at the conclusion of this faltering explanation. He struck his forehead. "If ever I heard of such a skip–brain! Having managed to get everything wrong side to, you go off and take the girl from the one place where she was perfectly safe and hand her over to Croil like a neatly wrapped box of bon-bons! Never mind, though; I think I know where to find her now."

And, whipping up his horses, he set off at a rapid pace down the road in the direction from which he had just come.

"But where are you going?" Geraint asked, bewildered.

He could not imagine in what way his account of how he had come to seek the Countess at Shoreham could have enlightened his cousin as to the course that the gang who had abducted her intended to take. But Jasper merely told him not to be a gudgeon.

"Of course that conversation Peggy overheard between Croil and your mother had nothing to do with *me*," he said. "They were discussing their own plans to abduct the Countess, and, since they spoke of taking her away by sea, I have a very good notion now of where to find her. There has been a small fishing lugger standing off Shoreham in a highly suspicious manner all day today — no doubt awaiting orders to sail with a very unusual cargo — and unless I am much mistaken, that is where that gang of ruffians has taken the Countess. It is a very easy matter, you know, to dispose of a body at sea."

"To dispose of a body!" Geraint stared over at his cousin, aghast. "But, Jasper, you *can't* mean — you can't possibly think — that Mama would — " He could not manage to get the words out, so shocked was he. "What possible reason could she have for wishing to harm the Countess?" he went on, after a moment.

And then, suddenly, as if in a lightning flash, he remembered the strange words the Countess had addressed to him just before her abductors had appeared: "I'm not a countess at all! I am an actress named Rolande Henry!" There was more of a mystery about the "Countess Môra," he realised now, than he had ever suspected. He turned a white face to his cousin.

"She told me — she told me," he stammered, "just before those men came, that she isn't a countess, that her name is Rolande Henry and she is an actress — Jasper, what *is* this all about? Who is she, really, and why do Mama and Croil want her out of the way?"

"Oh, they have some very good reasons for it," Jasper said grimly, "eight million of them, in point of fact." He went on, as Geraint merely looked more bewildered than ever. "Well, there's no use in my trying to fob you off any longer with Banbury tales; Croil knows very well who she is now — or he believes he knows, which makes matters even worse. And if you think what happened tonight is your fault, coz, you had best take heart, for if it hadn't been for *my* concocting the most birdwitted scheme imaginable to smoke out that bogus Giles Arcourt your clever mama was trying to foist upon us, Rolande would never have been in danger in the first place!"

He proceeded, as the curricle sped along the dark, empty road, to give Geraint a brief account of the plot he had devised to foil Lady Prest's attempt to pass off an imposter as the real Giles Arcourt and thus obtain control of the Arcourt fortune for herself and, eventurally, for Geraint.

Geraint sat stunned. He had long been vaguely and uncomfortably aware that his mama concealed behind a fragile and rigidly proper facade a will of iron and a total disregard for the rights and feelings of anyone but herself; but he could not believe, all in a single instant, that she could have been guilty of chicanery on such a vast scale, to say nothing of attempted murder. He would have liked to argue the matter with Jasper, and make at least an attempt to defend her, but when he looked at his cousin's face something told him it would be better not to.

So he sat in sick silence as Jasper drove the few miles back to Shoreham. Had he not been in such a state of shock, the mastery his cousin displayed in handling his team while racing at top speed over a shadowy, moonlit road must have filled him with admiration.

The scene, when they reached it, looked exactly the same as it had when he had driven Rolande away from it earlier in the night. The same half-intoxicated loiterer to whom he had given his phaeton in charge came shambling forward to perform a similar service for Jasper's curricle, his rheumy eyes widening in astonishment at sight of the curricle's occupants.

A rum go, he was obviously thinking as he attempted to clarify the situation in his somewhat befuddled mind. *First this flash cove drives up with a young gentry-mort and goes on board the* Swallow *with her. Then he leaves and this* second *flash cove drives up.*

He goes on board the Swallow, *too, and comes back with the young gentry-mort and drives her off. Twenty minutes later it's the first cove again; he boards the* Swallow, *comes back before the cat can lick her ear, and drives off in a tearing hurry. And now he's back again with the second cove, who looks like he's just come away from half a dozen rounds with Champion Tom Cribb —*

The first cove was putting a series of rapid questions to him, appearing ready to jump down his throat and extract the answers by main force if he was slow in replying. He gathered his clouded wits together, scenting largesse if he was prompt and willing.

Yes, he said, a closed carriage had driven down from the upper town not long ago. Yes, there had been several men inside. A lady? No — no lady. (Jasper and Geraint regarded each other, baffled.) Where had the men gone? Why, another cove had been a-waiting for them, it looked like; he came rowing up in a small boat and they all got in but the driver of the carriage, and were took out to that lugger that had been standing offshore all day. They had a heavy sack with them, he added helpfully; it had taken two of them to heave it aboard —

"A sack!" shouted Jasper, interrupting him. "Of course! Come along, Geraint!"

He tossed a coin to his informant and raced across to the *Swallow*, shouting to someone called Will: it turned out to be the burly man with whom Geraint had had the altercation earlier that night. In a space of seconds, it seemed to Geraint, whose mental processes had been so upset by the staggering revelations of the night that he now felt he was participating in a kind of nightmare in which logic was quite absent and one was merely rushed along from one lurid event to another without the slightest pause for reflection, he, Jasper, and the burly man were tumbling into a small boat; the burly man bent his back to the oars; and soon they were rapidly approaching the lugger, which lay quiet on the dark, gently rippling water before them.

"I know — that old boat," the burly man puffed, between strokes. "She's been smuggling rum — out of Holland — this many a long year. Charlie Spratt — he's the master — he'll turn his hand — to anything — if the price is right."

"They are armed, of course," Jasper said, interrupting him. "Damnation! I shall have to think of something, and quickly."

"Your young friend — he's got as nice a pop on him — as you'd like to see," the burly man placidly rejoined. "If it's wanting to have a quiet tell — with Charlie Spratt — you have in mind — just you let him cast his ogles on it. He won't want — no trouble — Charlie won't."

Jasper looked at Geraint. "*Have* you a pistol on you?" he enquired incredulously.

Geraint nodded.

"Good God!" said Jasper, as his young cousin handed the elegant, wicked-looking weapon over to him. "Who were you intending to shoot with this? Me? No, don't answer that; I don't want to be distracted." He slipped the pistol into his pocket and pulled out his purse. "Fifty pounds," he said, counting it. "A goodly sum, but I rather think that murder would have come

187

higher than that. What a pity I was depending on drawing on Foley's in Paris instead of carrying cash!'' He turned to Geraint. ''How much have you on you, coz?''

It developed that Geraint, who had already parted with a five-pound note to the burly man in the interests of obtaining the key to the cabin on the *Swallow*, had only seventeen pounds to contribute to the cause of bribery. By this time they were approaching the lugger, and a roughly dressed individual with a hoarse voice, leaning over the rail with a suspicious look on his face, demanded their business.

''We've come for the young lady,'' Jasper said amicably.

''What young lady?'' The hoarse-voiced man looked at him with increased suspicion.

''You know very well what young lady. The one you took out of the phaeton on the Brighton Road.''

''Ar-r,'' said the hoarse-voiced man, looking nonplussed.

''Ar-r indeed,'' said Jasper. He took the pistol out of his pocket; it glinted dangerously in the moonlight. ''I am accounted an excellent shot,'' he remarked conversationally,'' and I have unfortunately very few scruples about shooting people who have been hired to drop sacks containing young ladies into the sea at a safe distance from shore. On the other hand, not being of a bloodthirsty nature, I am quite willing to forget about shooting anyone at all, and on the contrary to bestow the considerable sum of sixty–seven pounds upon the person responsible for handing said young lady over to me.'' The hoarse-voiced man said nothing. ''Well? What about it?'' Jasper demanded.

The hoarse-voiced man, thus adjured, gave it as his opinion that nobody was going to hit nobody with a pistol from as unsteady a place as a little cockleshell a-bobbing up and down in the water, and added that, furthermore, if anybody tried to come aboard, he would find there were people who could fire off pistols themselves a-waiting to greet him.

"Nonsense!" said Jasper. "I have hit a Mahratta tribesman in India from the back of a galloping horse at thirty yards, so I shall certainly have no difficulty in blowing a hole through you at this trifling distance. And if you or your companions don't remain on deck to be shot at, you won't be able to stop us from boarding." The hoarse-voiced man looked dubious. "Sixty-seven pounds," said Jasper firmly. "That is my final offer. Take it or war will be declared."

The burly man, Will, unexpectedly added his voice to the negotiations at this point, advising the man on the lugger to give over talking silly blusteracious nonsense and give the gentleman what he was axing for.

"He'll be the cold death of you if you don't, Charlie Spratt," he said. "Lord love you, don't you see he's Quality, and ghastly proud Quality at that, and would give 'ee a bullet in the yed as soon as look at you? 'Ess fay, and sixty-seven pound in pocket do be sixty-seven pound, and murder do be murder, howsomever you may call it — "

The hoarse-voiced man said, albeit with a good deal less conviction now, that that was as might be, but the truth of it was that he had no young female aboard his vessel.

"Suppose you let us look, all the same," Jasper

13

said. "You might be surprised at what we find."

And before the hoarse-voiced man could utter a protest he was aboard the lugger, closely followed by Geraint, who was determined to be no whit behind in service to his lady.

The hoarse-voiced man, now supported by two cohorts who had apparently been skulking just out of sight on the companionway leading below, and who had sprung up, each brandishing a large pistol, took a belligerent step forward, as if to bar the way to the boarding party, but was immediately disarmed, metaphorically speaking, by Jasper's thrusting a large roll of banknotes into his hand. He did this with his left hand; in his right, he held Geraint's duelling pistol.

"Do you mind?" he asked, pointing it negligently in the direction of the sturdy ruffian who was standing at the head of the companionway, effectively barring his way below.

The man, with a glance at the master of the vessel, moved reluctantly aside, and Jasper went quickly down the steep companionway, followed at once by Geraint. He paused before the door below.

"Locked?" he debated. "Or is she being guarded?" He kept the pistol at the ready. "Try it, coz."

Geraint turned the handle of the door, which opened at once. The next moment he and Jasper stood confronting in high astonishment, in the light of a lantern suspended from a beam in the ceiling, a very white, very dishevelled, very determined Rolande, who faced them, holding a sort of small stiletto or dagger of some kind menacingly in her hand. She was in the very act, it seemed, of taking a swift step forward with obviously hostile intent when she recognised Geraint and, letting her weapon fall, flung herself into his arms instead.

"Oh, it's you!" she sobbed. "It *is* you! Oh, I *knew* you would come! Oh, Geraint, do take me away from this horrible boat! I have been in a sack, and they were planning to throw me overboard in it, only I cut my way out, because they didn't know I still had my reticule and there was a pair of scissors in it, and — and I've been so frightened! Oh, *do* take me away!"

Jasper, who was experiencing a strange, unpleasant, and altogether unexpected sensation, exactly as if someone had dealt him a violent blow in the pit of the stomach, took a step backward, out of the light, where he made a rapid effort to persuade himself that the decidedly uncomfortable feeling he had just experienced had nothing at all to do with the sight of Miss Rolande Henry throwing herself, with every appearance of passionate abandon, into his young cousin's arms.

SIXTEEN

The remainder of the night, to Rolande at least, passed like a sort of sleep-walker's dream. She was bundled off the lugger into a small boat and rowed ashore; she was lifted tenderly by Geraint into Jasper's curricle and driven rapidly back to Brighton; she was received by the Baroness into the house on the Steyne with all the solicitude and relief occasioned by the horrid hours of speculation she had spent following her discovery of the note Jasper had left explaining his intention to remove Rolande to France. Here she was put to bed at once, and fell almost immediately into a deep sleep; and although she awoke several times with a terrified start, feeling herself once more stifled by the coarse burlap of the sack that had been flung over her by her abductors, she was quickly reassured by the feel of a luxurious featherbed and linen sheets and promptly fell asleep again.

Of course the Baroness had to hear the whole story from Jasper that very night — or, rather, dawn, for by that time the midsummer sun was rising cheerfully in a cloudless sky. Geraint had gone home, but Jasper, declaring that it was his intention to take up residence in the house as long as Rolande remained there, the better to keep her under surveillance, had sent to the Old Ship for his gear. In the meantime, he was quite willing to sit drinking coffee with the Baroness in the morning-parlour and discussing the events of the night with her. He looked, the Baroness thought, unusually subdued for Jasper, but she put it down to his having passed an anxious and strenuous night.

"What pleases me most of all," she said, when she had wrung most of the details of the night's adventures from him, "is that Rolande was so very intelligent as to succeed in getting herself out of the sack those horrid men had put her into. So clever of her, don't you think, to remember the scissors in her reticule? — to say nothing of her brilliant notion of taking them apart to make a dagger. I daresay one might very well kill a man with such a weapon, and it is exceedingly regrettable that she did not; only I expect it might have been a rather disagreeable experience, after all. But what are we to do with her now? You were quite right, it seems, in thinking that Croil and Honoria are convinced that the Countess Móra is actually the Giles Arcourt you had staying with you at Arcourt's Hall — "

"Yes, they are convinced of that," Jasper said grimly. "And before another four-and-twenty hours have passed they will be convinced of something else as well — and that is that if any further attempts are made on Miss Henry's life they will find themselves in the dock at the Old Bailey. I wasn't in a position tonight to obtain information as to who had paid them from that crew of ruffians who abducted her, but I know who the men are, and even if they have gone off to France or to Holland I shall put Birdwhistell on to tracing them and they will certainly be found and induced to give evidence. With *that* threat held over her head, I don't think even the lure of eight million pounds will be enough to bring my dear aunt to risk another attack upon Miss Henry." He made a grimace of distaste. "It makes my blood run cold to think I am related to such a creature!" he said. "She was born several hundred years too late, you know. I am sure she would have enjoyed the company of such high-born ladies as Lucrezia Borgia and that charming queen of England who plotted with her lover to put her husband, the king, out of the way — Edward II, wasn't it?"

The Baroness said how odd, for she believed it was actually true that, on the mother's side, his and Honoria's branch of the Arcourts was connected with the French princess whom Edward II had married — "which probably explains everything," she said, with an air of satisfaction.

Privately, she also found it rather odd that Jasper was now saying nothing about taking Rolande off to France for safety, which, as he had bought a yacht especially for that purpose, seemed rather improvident to her. But, upon second thought, it occurred to her that he might well consider that, after the girl's harrowing experience with boats, it might be difficult to induce her to board one again; also that he probably felt secure in his belief that Honoria would not be bold enough to make any further attempts upon Rolande's life in the face of the threat he was now able to hold over her.

Actually, however, there was still a further consideration behind Jasper's decision to allow Rolande to remain in Brighton for the present. The manner in which she had behaved towards Geraint and he towards her had convinced him that they were passionately attached to each other, and that Geraint, in spite of his mother's opposition and his knowledge of the Countess Móra's true identity, would make her an offer of marriage at the earliest opportunity. Jasper, who had never had the faintest notion of offering marriage to anyone himself, and on the whole had always thought poorly of young men who walked into parson's mouse-trap of their own free will, was trying hard to adopt this attitude towards his cousin Geraint's obvious inclination to get himself leg-shackled. But he found himself falling instead into a very morose and belligerent state of mind, so that he looked forward almost with pleasure to his forthcoming interview with Croil and his aunt Honoria, as giving him an opportunity to vent his disagreeable feelings upon someone else. When his nightgear arrived from the Old Ship, he went up to the bedchamber the Baroness had had prepared for him to try to snatch a few hours' sleep, but succeeded in doing no more than falling into a fitful and highly unsatisfactory doze, from which he awakened with the feeling that some dark tragedy was closing inevitably in upon him.

He got up in a very ill humour, dressed, and went off to call upon his aunt Honoria.

Shortly afterwards Rolande, too, awoke, and, feeling it necessary to seek the reassurance of company, quickly dressed and went downstairs to find the Baroness. She had not allowed Disbrey to make her up as the Countess Móra in another of the Baroness's black wigs, being convinced that, as her disguise had now been penetrated, there was no point in her trying to pretend to be anyone but herself, and she looked rather odd but very charming, with her own boyish crop, in a cherry-striped gown of French muslin.

But the Baroness, she found, was not available for conversation, having gone off to bed to try to make up for some of the sleep she had lost. Rolande wandered disconsolately into the drawing room. She found it very depressing that no one appeared to wish to talk to her about her narrow escape from death, and she was wondering, besides, what would happen to her now. Obviously she could not continue living any longer with the Baroness as the Countess Móra, and she considered it highly probable that Jasper had not abandoned his scheme to carry her off to a place of safety in France. He had behaved very strangely to her, she thought, on the drive back to Brighton the previous night, speaking only in monosyllables and scarcely appearing in the least pleased or relieved that her abductors had not succeeded in carrying out their horrid plan of dropping her into the sea. No doubt he was still very angry with her for having gone off from the *Swallow* with Geraint — and rightly so, she was forced to admit, for if she had remained aboard the yacht she would have been perfectly safe, and he would not have been obliged to take enormous risks in order to rescue her.

As to exactly what those risks had been she was still not very clear, but she had gathered from Geraint's excited and disjointed conversation on the drive back to Brighton, as he had sat perched up behind her in the groom's seat between the springs, that it had been Jasper's that had been the master-mind behind her rescue, and that, if he had not managed the matter so coolly, he would have stood in great danger of being killed himself.

"I have caused him nothing but trouble from start to finish," she thought, in the melancholy frame of mind induced by frayed nerves — a state quite foreign to her usual optimistic nature. "I daresay he wishes he had never set eyes on me. But I shall make it up to him!"

For there was no real reason, she thought, why she could not now go back to being Giles Arcourt again — which was who Croil and Lady Prest certainly believed her to be. And if, as Jasper seemed so convinced he would be, Lady Prest's Giles Arcourt were to be found and induced to continue putting forward his claim to the Arcourt fortune, she could then save the day for Jasper just as he had originally planned, after which, without even accepting the ten thousand pounds that had been offered her, she would return to her obscure life as an actress in France, cherishing the knowledge that it was through her that the man she loved was now in the enjoyment of one of the largest fortunes in England.

The touching scene of self-abnegation this conjured up — of herself standing sadly on the deck of the Calais packet, straining her eyes for a last glimpse of England, where at that very moment Jasper, now secure in his fortune, would probably be standing before the altar of St. George's, Hanover Square, with the bride of his choice (she envisioned Peggy Falkirk in this role) — had brought real tears to her eyes when Hendon entered to announce Lord Prest.

"Oh, do show him in," said Rolande, cheering up at once at the thought of having someone with whom she could discuss her adventures of the previous night.

Hendon went out, and in a few moments Geraint, looking almost as excited as he had the night before when he had assisted in her rescue, walked into the room.

"Good afternoon, Countess —" he began impetuously.

"Miss Henry," said Rolande.

Geraint, obviously put off his stride by this interruption, checked himself, blinking.

"It is 'Miss Henry,' not 'Countess,' " Rolande repeated scrupulously. "I told you so last night, you will remember." She regarded him curiously. "How warm you look!" she said. "And very much — *distrait* — "

"Do I?" said Geraint. "Well, yes, I daresay I do." He looked at her with a half-embarrassed, half-triumphant expression upon his face. "To tell you the truth, Miss Henry," he said, "I have had the most almighty brangle with my mother, and I have just left home — that is, the house she hired here for the summer — and taken rooms at the Old Ship. And what is more, I don't intend to go back!"

"Splendid!" said Rolande, in warm approval. "I think you have done exactly right! Do sit down and tell me all about it."

She seated herself upon a small satinwood tête-à-tête, but Geraint, who was obviously far too excited to do anything so tame as sitting down, remained on his feet while he described to her the events that had taken place that morning at his mama's house on the Marine Parade.

"Of course you know what Jasper says — that it is she and Croil who were behind that attempt on your life last night," he said. "Well, I put it to her — "

"You didn't!" Rolande said, in incredulous admiration. She remembered the way Geraint had always deferred to his imperious mama — it had seemed to her at times as if he scarcely dared to breathe without her permission — and thought, with her French practicality, that falling in love with the Countess Móra had done wonders for him. No doubt he would now be able some day to marry someone whom he really cared for, and lead a life of his own, instead of being presented with a bride of Lady Prest's choosing who would be as much under the latter's thumb as Geraint had always been. "What did she say?" she asked.

Geraint said he couldn't quite recollect her exact words, but she had been perfectly furious and had denied everything. She had also said some very cutting things about both Jasper and the Countess Móra, but before he could properly resent them the conversation had unfortunately been interrupted by the unexpected reappearance of Giles Arcourt.

Rolande sat up straighter. "Oh! Do you mean he has come back?" she demanded.

"Yes, he's come back," said Geraint, with a look of distaste. "He seems to have gone no farther than

Dover. I suspect it was one of Croil's agents who persuaded him — or perhaps coerced him — into returning: he arrived in company with an extraordinarily rum-looking fellow who didn't actually have him by the collar but looked as if he would have if he made one false move. Of course Mama was delighted to see him, but I told her that if anything more was wanted to convince me he was an imposter it was his snivelling, hangdog air — really, one *can't* believe any Arcourt could have sired such a puppy as that! And then," continued Geraint, with an air of daring the lightning, "I told her I was leaving, because I wanted no more to do with the whole despicable business, and she said, in that composed, icy way of hers, 'You may go, Geraint, but you will certainly come back,' and I said I wouldn't, and then I want off to the Old Ship."

Geraint paused for breath and also for applause, which he received unstintingly from Rolande. But in spite of her outward enthusiasm for the courage and initiative Geraint had displayed, she was inwardly much preoccupied with the news of Giles Arcourt's return. Obviously, Jasper's prediction had come true, and, notwithstanding her and the Baroness's plot to frighten the boy away, he was now once more very much in the picture and could be used by Lady Prest just as she had planned when she had first brought him to London.

This left Rolande in the situation she had been envisioning a little earlier in her lugubrious reflections on her future, and she determined, in self-sacrificial zeal, to do her utmost to convince Jasper, as soon as she saw him, that she was not only willing but determined to remain in England and play her role as Giles Arcourt out to the end for his benefit.

Occupied with these plans, she scarcely attended to what her present visitor was saying, and was very much startled to find him all at once down on his knees before her, clasping her hands fervently in his.

"Miss Henry! Rolande! You *did* say your name was Rolande, didn't you?" he broke off to ask, anxious lest he should have erred upon a point of such importance.

Rolande said that was indeed her name and, endeavouring to withdraw her hands from his grasp, requested him in a rather agitated voice to rise from his knees. She was in no condition at that moment, she felt, to cope with a proposal of marriage, and was a trifle apprehensive that she might even be led, by the dismal prospects she had just been envisioning for her own future, to forget her noble plans for helping Jasper to his fortune and accede to her young lover's importunities.

Not that she wished in the least to do so, but human nature was human nature, and she was feeling particularly low-spirited and friendless at that moment. Under such circumstances, one never knew how weak one might be.

Geraint, of course, did *not* rise from his knees, nor did he release her hands; instead, he covered them with kisses.

"Rolande!" he began unsteadily. "Since the first moment I met you I have loved — "

"What the *devil* are you doing?" an acerbic voice

broke in suddenly upon this romantically intended speech.

Geraint leaped to his feet. Rolande's cheeks flamed scarlet as her eyes flew to the door. It was, of course, Jasper who stood on the threshold, regarding them both with an ironical gaze.

"I — I — " Geraint stammered, almost overcome by equal parts of embarrassment and resentment, "I was — I was just — "

"You were just about to offer marriage to Miss Henry," Jasper finished it for him with brutal frankness. "Very well, then — if that is what you feel you must do, for God's sake do it; but don't eat the girl up before you have spoken your lines to her!"

"You — you — !" Geraint interrupted him furiously. He was very fond of his dashing cousin and admired him enormously; but it was the outside of enough, he felt, for him to be giving him lessons in love-making before his inamorata. "It's easy enough for you to carp and criticise, you — you libertine!" he went on, quite carried away by his embarrassment and rage. "*You* have had so much experience — "

"On the contrary," said Jasper, "I have had no experience at all. I have never offered marriage to a female in my life — but if I had, I shouldn't have gone about it in that cowhanded way! Look here, now —" He walked over to Rolande, who was still sitting frozen on the tête-à-tête, and, gently taking her hands, raised her so that she stood facing him, supported by one muscular arm that had passed itself masterfully about her waist. "You might proceed like this," he advised, and, brushing the lightest of kisses first on the amazed Rolande's coppery hair and then on her nose and parted lips, he said to her in a lowered, husky, tender voice, "Darling Miss Henry, my own true love — *will* you marry me?"

What reply he was anticipating from Rolande there was no way for either her or Geraint to know, but very probably it was not the one he received. Rolande stepped back, tore herself from his embrace, and administered a resounding box on his ear. At the same moment, or as nearly so as made no difference, she burst into tears, and retreating to the satinwood tête-à-tête, flung herself down upon it and began to sob as if her heart would break.

"You brute!" ejaculated Geraint, overcome by outraged sympathy for his beloved. "Now see what you have done!"

And, rushing to Rolande's side, he endeavoured to take her in his arms and soothe her, only to be driven off by the same unfriendly treatment Jasper had just received. Slightly staggered by a hearty box on the ear, he retreated smartly, fetching up against Jasper, who was still nursing his own stinging ear.

Rolande, meanwhile, conquering her sobs sufficiently to be able to speak, rounded with flashing eyes upon Jasper, quite ignoring Geraint; indeed, her attack upon the latter appeared to have been merely a reflex action, so to speak, reflecting no actual animus against him.

"I was *going*," she announced, with a fury slightly impeded by an occasional irrepressible sob, "to t-tell you that I w-wanted to stay in England so I c-could p-pretend to be Giles Arcourt again and g-get your b-beastly fortune for you; but now I w-wouldn't — n-not for anything! You n-needn't wish to m-marry me — that is your p-privilege; *ça se voit*! But to m-make game of me — !''

Hendon trod in stately fashion into the room.

''Mr. Birdwhistell!'' he announced; and the next moment the plump little lawyer himself impetuously hurried in.

''Mr. Carrington — my dear sir, you must forgive the intrusion, but they told me at your lodgings that I should find you here!'' he said in tones of pleasurable agitation, speaking before he had well had time to take in the interesting tableau that confronted him. ''Good news, one feels, need not stand upon ceremony, and I am delighted — most delighted! — to be able to report to you that our man has located the genuine Schmidts in Vienna, and along with them, the most unimpeachable documentary proof that you are without the shadow of a doubt the true legal heir to the Arcourt fortune!''

SEVENTEEN

To say that Mr. Birdwhistell's statement created the sensation he had obviously hoped for would be a gross exaggeration of the facts. Geraint, to whom at the moment the Arcourt fortune meant nothing at all, merely stared at him in an unfriendly manner; Rolande, whose passionate speech of recrimination to Jasper had been interrupted by the solicitor's entrance, found her handkerchief and sniffed vengefully into it; and Jasper, from whom Mr. Birdwhistell had hopefully expected the most, was regarding him, it seemed, with a strangely preoccupied expression upon his face. He looked rather, Mr. Birdwhistell thought, with a feeling of slight affront, as if he had something far more important on his mind than a matter of a mere eight million pounds.

Under such circumstances, it was Mr. Birdwhistell himself who felt it necessary to break the silence that his entering speech had caused.

"My dear Mr. Carrington, can it be that you do not take my meaning?" he enquired, his mild face looking more than ever like that of a scholarly country clergyman in the act of reproving a member of his flock for inattention to the sermon. "Klug — he is the former K.G.L. man whom I sent to Vienna, you know — has just returned with a complete documentary evidence that your young cousin, Giles Arcourt, indeed died in that city at the age of three, so that you are most indubitably left the heir to the Arcourt fortune! The matter developed, you see, exactly as I had hoped: Klug was able to track down these Schmidts with really extraordinary rapidity and obtain their confidence as one of their own order, and so to learn from them that the child left in their care by the Dubruls had died of the same fever that had carried off the Dubruls themselves. Terrified," Mr. Birdwhistell went on, warming to his theme, "terrified, I say, lest blame for this misfortune be placed at their door — for they had been convinced, you must know, both by the documents left with them by the Dubruls and by the expensive clothing of the child, that he was a member of a wealthy and important English family — they allowed the child to be buried as an Austrian waif whom they had befriended, and thereafter, when enquiries were made, denied ever having had the least knowledge either of the Dubruls or of the child who had been in their care. Most fortunately, however, they did not destroy the documents or the clothing — God bless my soul!" he broke off his narrative to ejaculate suddenly. His eyes were fixed upon Rolande, whom, in his zeal to communicate his good news to Jasper, he had scarcely glanced at up to this time. "Who is this?" he demanded, curiosity and astonishment for once getting the better of his customary old-fashioned courtesy.

"May I present my solicitor, Mr. Birdwhistell — Miss Henry," Jasper said punctiliously.

He appeared to have recovered from his fit of absent-mindedness; in fact, there was now a gleam of more than usual animation in his eyes.

"But surely — surely," Mr. Birdwhistell stammered, still regarding Rolande with a transfixed expression upon his face, "surely we have met before, Miss — er — Henry? I feel I cannot be mistaken — "

"Giles Arcourt — Arcourt's Hall," Jasper obligingly refreshed his memory. "At that time, you see, owing to circumstances beyond her control, Miss Henry was being a young man. I shan't go into detail, but I am sure I may rely on your discretion, Birdwhistell, to cause you to forget that you had ever met Miss Henry before you entered this room. She is, by the bye, to my knowledge and her own, no connexion of the late Mrs. John Arcourt's, in spite of the rather striking resemblance between them — "

"Striking — yes, yes, striking indeed!" said Mr. Birdwhistell, still looking most bewildered by this turn of events. "And of course, my dear boy, you may rely on me to say nothing of my previous meeting with — with Miss Henry. But how — but why — ?"

"It is all really quite simple," Jasper explained, realising that he would be obliged to give some account of the matter to the bemused solicitor or see him burst with curiosity before his very eyes. "I have always heard, you see, that the best way to fight fire is with fire, so I took a leaf from my clever aunt Honoria's book and dug up an imposter of my own — "

The expression of bemused bewilderment upon Mr. Birdwhistell's benevolent face slowly altered as he took in the meaning of this statement: the corners of the small mouth, which had been open in an "O" of astonishment, curved slightly upward; a light of innocent glee appeared and grew in his mild blue eyes.

"Oh, excellent! Capital! Capital!" he pronounced, rubbing his hands together in high appreciation. "Really an extraordinarily clever plan, dear boy; I should never have imagined you capable of such a stratagem! And you cozened me nicely, you know — very nicely! — when I saw the young man — the young lady," he corrected himself, bowing to Rolande, "at Arcourt's Hall, with your talk of your suspicions of him! Dear me! Dear me!"

And he regarded Jasper with an expression of such warm approval in his eyes that Jasper, somewhat startled by this unexpected evidence of a Machiavellian turn of mind in his highly respectable solicitor, began to wonder if this sort of thing was not the sole prerogative of Croil, but belonged instead to the entire profession. He had had a very satisfactory but not quite conclusive conversation that day with Croil, whom he had found in his aunt Honoria's house on the Marine Parade, together with a sullen and obviously frightened "Giles Arcourt," and his rejoicing, from a personal point of view, over the news that Mr. Birdwhistell had brought was at the moment as nothing in comparison with his pleasure in the knowledge that any lingering plans Croil and Lady Prest might still have for obtaining the Arcourt fortune and harming Rolande would now be forever overset by Mr. Birdwhistell's discoveries.

Wishing to be properly grateful to Mr. Birdwhistell, he therefore put aside his own immediate inclination, which was to get him and Geraint out of the house as soon as possible, and instead invited him to sit down and tell him all about Klug's adventures. This Mr. Birdwhistell was only too happy to do. Rolande and Geraint, however, showed an extraordinary lack of interest in this gripping tale, the former continuing to sit with a vengeful expression upon her face, although she had stopped crying, and the latter obviously simmering with impatience.

When at last the solicitor had told his whole (and, as it seemed to them, interminable) tale and had taken his departure, they scarcely waited for the door to close behind him before they both fell upon Jasper and took up their unfinished business with him where Mr. Birdwhistell had interrupted it.

"I *don't* wish to be uncivil, coz," Geraint said urgently, "and I do congratulate you most sincerely upon your good fortune, but you *must* see I should like to be private now with Miss Henry."

At the same moment that he began to speak, Rolande also commenced what appeared to be a hostilely intended speech to Jasper, but, being overborne by her suitor's agitated words, was obliged to content herself with inimical mutterings as she bided her time and awaited her own opportunity to be heard.

For his part, Jasper appeared quite unperturbed by the coldness of the atmosphere that surrounded him, and, replying to Geraint at once in an affable voice, said that if he wished to make an offer to Miss Henry he, Jasper, would be happy to wait until he had done so, but that as he himself had something of the same sort in mind, he thought he had better not go away.

"You have *what*?" Geraint said, looking completely stunned.

As for Rolande, she thought she might be going to faint. She told herself that she could not possibly have heard what she had thought she had, and wondered wildly for a moment if the strain upon her nerves of the past night's adventures had been such that she was now subject to hallucinations.

Jasper, however, now repeated his incredible statement.

"I said I have it in mind to make a declaration to Miss Henry myself," he said. "So if you don't mind, coz, will you get on with yours, as I find myself growing more impatient moment by moment?"

Geraint, now looking extremely red and embarrassed, said stiffly that if Jasper had the least degree of delicacy, he would understand that no man could make such a declaration in the presence of a third person.

"I expect I haven't any at all, then," Jasper said equably, "— delicacy, that is — because I can see no difficulty whatever in the matter. Darling Miss Henry," he went on, approaching Rolande and, as she gazed up at him in a mesmerised fashion, drawing her once more to her feet, just as he had done before Mr. Birdwhistell's arrival, "darling Miss Henry, *will* you marry me? Improbable as it seems, I really mean it, and if your answer is *No* I shall undoubtedly go off into a decline, like the young ladies in the sentimental novels, because I love vou — I love you — I love you — I love you."

And with each reiteration of the words he dropped a moth-kiss upon hair and brow and nose and lips.

His arms were around her, or Rolande was quite certain now that she would have fainted. But even in the midst of the turmoil of hope and doubt in her mind, she still had a thought for poor Geraint, and stretched out a hand to him consolingly.

"*Mon pauvre!*" she said to him unsteadily. "You must go away; you must go at once and forget all about me — "

"But I love you, too!" Geraint exclaimed fiercely. "You *can't* send me away! Besides, he is only trifling with you! He don't really wish to marry you!"

"Now there," said Jasper fair-mindedly, "you wrong me, coz. Not only do I *wish* to marry Miss Henry; I am determined to do so, even if she refuses to have me." He looked down at Rolande, still holding her in his arms. "*Are* you going to have me, darling Miss Henry?" he enquired. "It will make matters so much simpler, you know, because I shall have unlimited funds now and can pursue you to the ends of the earth if you choose to flee from me."

Rolande had by this time recovered herself slightly, and had decided — not very sensibly, but in her present addled state of mind sense was scarcely to be expected of her — that all that was happening was merely a plot of Jasper's, designed to cause her to reject Geraint's offer. If she could have brought herself to do so, she would have been exceedingly happy to thwart him by accepting Geraint; but she could not and would not do this, knowing that she would undoubtedly jilt him as soon as they had become properly engaged.

So she contented herself instead with wriggling with what dignity she could out of Jasper's embrace and saying sympathetically to Geraint, "I know you think now that you love me, *mon pauvre*, but you have known me, after all, only for a very short time. And I am quite, *quite* sure that you will think differently of me — oh, perhaps even before the summer has passed! We should not suit in the least, you know."

"No, I should rather think not," Jasper agreed, breaking, in a most improper way, into a conversation in which he was obviously not intended to be included. "As a matter of fact, coz, I can tell you that you would certainly find yourself living under the cat's foot if you were so unwise as to marry Miss Henry; why, I shouldn't wonder if it wouldn't be almost as bad as living with your mother! Miss Henry has a very warm temper, you know; there is too much red in that hair by far to promise any man a quiet life. And you have just seen for yourself that she can even become violent upon occasion — "

It is doubtful that Geraint attended to this — as Rolande considered — highly unjustified and callous speech sufficiently to take in its meaning; he was gazing instead despairingly into Rolande's face. Indubitably, it appeared very kind and sympathetic, but at the same time it had so unalterable a look of finality about it that he found himself unable to cling any longer to the hope that there would ever be any warmer expression of feeling in it for him. With a gesture that was probably meant to indicate love's despair, but instead managed to convey only a very young man's disappointment and chagrin, he walked quickly from the room.

Jasper clicked his tongue. "Fie upon you, Miss Henry; now see what you have done!" he said reprovingly. "After all, he has loved you for three whole days together, to quote one of my favourite poets — "

Rolande turned to him, her eyes flashing.

"How *dare* you make game of the poor boy?" she exclaimed. "*He* is sincere in saying that he cares for me, at any rate!"

"Well, he can't be any more sincere than I am," Jasper said, advancing upon her with the obvious intention of taking her once more into his arms. She placed herself strategically behind the satinwood tête-à-tête. "I don't know why you won't believe me," he complained, regarding her with some severity. "Haven't I conducted myself in the approved style of ardent lovers, rescuing you from dire perils at the risk of my own life, being prepared to give you up to a worthier man when I thought he was the one you really care for — ? Do you know what sort of unmitigated hell you put me through, darling Miss Henry, when you flung yourself so enthusiastically into Geraint's arms last night on that blasted boat? I give you my word, it was like having Gentleman Jackson land me a settler in the ring, and I never had another cheerful thought until I walked in here and saw my young cousin on his knees before you, and you looking as if you would have given any amount of money to anyone who would take him by the ear and lead him gently but firmly out of the room — "

Rolande, from behind the tête-à-tête, was still regarding him suspiciously.

"I don't believe you!" she said. "You — you told me once, when we were at Arcourt's Hall, that you wished to marry a meek female of a conformable nature, and that is not at all a proper description of me! And you told Geraint just now that I am bad-tempered, and not at all the sort of person one would wish for a wife —"

"You *are* rather bad-tempered sometimes," Jasper said. "So am I. And it is quite true that you are not at all the wife for Geraint; but, on the other hand, I know now that I was abysmally mistaken when I said I should like a conformable spouse, and that *you* are exactly the wife to suit me. I can't think, in fact, why you don't see that yourself, for you told me at Arcourt's Hall, I recall very clearly, that you wished to marry a man *tout à fait sympathique,* who would be excessively fond of you and anxious to do everything possible to please you — which certainly nicks the nick as far as my feelings are concerned. And then you added that it would do me a great deal of good to be married to a lady of an over-bearing disposition, which should assuredly settle the matter — "

"I am *not* overbearing!" said Rolande hotly; but she was obliged to break off as Jasper again exhibited unmistakable signs of an intention to come to closer quarters with her.

No doubt it was his superior footwork, developed

in a good many hours of sparring with Gentleman Jackson in the latter's well-known Boxing Saloon in Bond Street, that enabled him to get behind the satin-wood tête-à-tête before she could succeed in whipping round to the other side, as she no doubt had had every intention of doing. At any rate, she found herself once more in his embrace and this time it was a far more ruthless and powerful one than it had been when Geraint had been in the room. The same could also be said of the kiss that was pressed upon her lips — no moth-kiss now, but one that left her blissful and shaken, as if some happy cataclysm had passed over her.

"You see, my darling, darling Rolande, I really have developed a *grande passion* for you, after all," Jasper said presently, in a voice that sounded no steadier than she felt. "And you *must* believe me when I tell you so, because if you don't, I shall never leave off kissing you — which doesn't seem a bad idea, after all," he concluded, renewing the actions that had caused the happy cataclysm, with much the same results. "*Will* you marry me?" he broke off at last to demand.

"But—*bien entendu*! Of course!" Rolande said, on a long, contented sigh. And then considering, with her French wisdom, that in spite of everything it would not do to make it all that easy for him, she added demurely, "You could not possibly contrive to spend eight million pounds all alone, you know!"

It was at that moment that the Baroness walked into the room.

You may felicitate me, Cousin Louisa," Jasper

said, glancing over his shoulder at her without releasing his promised bride. "Birdwhistell has discovered that I am beyond the shadow of a doubt the heir to the Arcourt fortune, and Rolande has agreed to marry me so that she may help spend it."

The Baroness's beady black eyes, darting swiftly to Rolande's blissful face, then returned at once, with an air of great satisfaction, to Jasper.

"Dearest Jasper," she said, "I could not possibly be happier for you and for dear Rolande. She has been in love with you, of course, since she first clapped eyes on you, and I am very glad that you have finally realised that you are in love with her as well. *So* tiresome to watch you pretending to yourself that she was merely a tribulation to you, when all the while it was quite obvious to anyone of experience that you had fallen top-over-tail in love for the very first time in your life. I must say I almost despaired for a time of your ever having sufficient sense to ask her to marry you, and had made definite plans to have her become Lady Hoult. Men are so stupid in matters of this sort — don't you agree, my dear?" she asked Rolande.

Rolande said indignantly that she didn't think Jasper was stupid in the least, and certainly no one could blame him for not realising he was in love with her, because she had been playing so many different roles during the past few weeks that it must have been rather like falling in love with a chameleon.

"Well — perhaps," the Baroness conceded tolerantly. "But to prove my point in another way, my dear, there is that mooncalf Geraint, whom I came across in the hall just now looking as if the world had collapsed around his ears. Of course I realised at once that you must have refused him, so I gave him a severe lecture on the folly of falling in love with mysterious countesses who turned out not to be countesses at all, and represented to him how very much more suitable it would be if he were to fix his affections on some young lady from his own circle. 'There is Kitty Wentworth,' I said to him. 'She has been absolutely love-sick for you these three months, and is really a quite delightful girl, to say nothing of being far prettier than Rolande.' It cheered him up amazingly; there is nothing more salutory for people who had been disappointed in love, you see, than to find there is someone dying of love for *them*. I shouldn't wonder if the two of them would make a match of it in the end, which will be an excellent thing, as she is a girl of spirit, and quite able, I should think, to hold her own with Honoria. Now if only there were something I could do to get poor Peggy out of Honoria's clutches — "

"Cousin Louisa," said Jasper, who had been attending with signs of obvious impatience to the Baroness's discursive speech, "if I tell you that it is my intention to provide Peggy with a suitable competence, so that she will be able to live apart from Aunt Honoria, in recognition of my gratitude to her for having helped me to rescue Rolande, will you go away and leave us alone? I know you are fond of arranging people's lives, but I can assure you that Rolande and I really need no assistance from you at this point."

The Baroness, instead of being affronted, laughed, and tapped him meaningly on the arm.

"But certainly, dearest Jasper!" she said. "I quite

understand!" She turned towards the door, and then abruptly turned back again. "It has just occurred to me to wonder," she said impressively, "*what* are we to say to people when they observe — as I rather think they must — the unusual resemblance between your bride and the 'Countess Móra'? It is really rather awkward — "

"Not at all!" said Jasper, with aplomb. "I shall merely explain that it was this resemblance to the Countess, for whom, as is well known, I had conceived a *grande passion* but who unfortunately was out of my sphere, that initially attracted me to Miss Henry and led to my subsequent marriage to her. I shall further explain," he went on, gazing down at Rolande, whom he continued to hold firmly in his arms, "that, devoted as I am to my wife, she will never be able to mean to me what the Countess did — "

"You won't!" said Rolande indignantly, but found her protest stopped by a kiss.

The Baroness, perceiving that a lovers' quarrel was in progress, gave the two of them a final look of approval out of her beady black eyes and whisked herself quickly out of the room.

All Futura Books are available at your bookshop or newsagent, or can be ordered from the following address:
Futura Books, Cash Sales Department,
P.O. Box 11, Falmouth, Cornwall.

Please send cheque or postal order (no currency), and allow 30p for postage and packing for the first book plus 15p for the second book and 12p for each additional book ordered up to a maximum charge of £1.29 in U.K.

Customers in Eire and B.F.P.O. please allow 30p for the first book, 15p for the second book plus 12p per copy for the next 7 books, thereafter 6p per book.

Overseas customers please allow 50p for postage and packing for the first book and 10p per copy for each additional book.